NCM Publishing Presents

SLEEPING *In* SIN

CORNELIA SMITH

PUBLISHER'S NOTE:
This book is a work of fiction. Names, Characters, Places, and incidents either are products of the author's imagination or are used fictitiously. Any resemblance to actual events or locales or persons, living or dead, is pure and entirely coincidental.

Sleeping in Sin
Written by: Cornelia Smith
Edited by: Caitlin Bailey, Andre Eaton
Text Formation: Write On Promotions
Cover Design and Layout: Trendsetters Publications Inc. Creative
www.ncmpublishing.com

ACKNOWLEDGMENTS

To my sisters you are the mirror that exposes my scars and the bed I lay in to heal. the bond we share I cherish its a big deal. To my best friend and sister in crime, Jessica I thank you for your support.

Last but never least, I thank God for my struggles, the only motivation a girl from an urban up bringing has for hope and to my new readers enjoy. & To Ni'cola, I thank you for the opportunity. Love you momma (Nita) dear Muah!

DEDICATION

This book is dedicated to my struggles. I will continue to use my scars for strength and for a map to my future success. God Bless

Sleeping

In Sin

From: Author

C. Smith

To: My great Readers
@ MLK ♡

Khalon: The Great Detective

The 6'1" built butterscotch brown skin detective arrived at the crime scene shaking his head, his long dreads shaking from side-to-side as he realizes the identity of the victim. "Officer, do we have a time of death?" he asked the skinny, white rookie cop.

"Yes detective, 11:00 p.m."

"Is there a witness?"

"No sir," The cop said, shaking his head, taking a deep breath like he wished there was.

"Okay, I will take it from here, thanks." Khalon walked around the crime scene watching his steps, making sure he didn't step on any valuable evidence.

"Detective, would you like me to contact the victim's family?"

"No, I got it officer. This one is personal."

"Understood, I didn't know you knew the victim."

"Yeah, we were raised in the same neighborhood growing up. He was a good kid."

"My kids loved his music, but I personally didn't listen to it." Detective Khalon patted the rookie cop on the shoulders.

"Naw, I wouldn't expect you to officer-- what is it?-- John?" Khalon looked at the white officer, reading his badge, and then looked back at the rapper Kilo's body, shaking his head. "Damn boy, your mother is going to have a fit once she hears about this," Khalon mumbled to himself while whiping his face taking a deep breath in and out. After ten seconds of silence Khalon, patted the rookie on his upper back, before walking off snapping "Officer John, make sure this body gets handled with care and tell the news nothing until we can get a lead on this thing."

"Yes sir, will do."

Khalon jumped in his black charger that he was given for being the best cop of the year. He never drove any of his luxury cars to work knowing that the work would put his babies in harm's way. While driving down Charleston Khalon thought to himself, what am I going to tell this lady about her only baby boy? You would think after ten years of experience that I would be great with this. Khalon was pulling up to Kilo's mother, subdivision and his time was running out. "Damn, here comes hell," Khalon uttered after shutting his car door. Very hesitantly, Khalon, walked around the nicely cut grass up to the stairs. His heart began to beat faster than a running horse. The knocks on the door were soft and everlasting.

"Ah right already I'm coming, I'm coming."

"Hello Ms. White, how are you?"

"Am fine and you?"

Before Khalon could give Ms. White an answer to her question, she cut him off with amazement that he was at her door. "WOW! What are doing at my door? I hear you are the best cop in New York these days."

Blushing, Khalon responded. "Well, I try my best."

"That's good, baby. Well come on in, what can I do for you?" Ms. White cut him off again while she went on rambling. You could see Khalon dimple from his semi-smile as he noticed that Ms. White could still talk up a storm.

"I remember you when you were a lil boy running around Marcy like you owned the place, you and that no good friend of yours. I must say though, I always thought you were going to be the trouble kid. As much trouble you use to get into," Ms. White said while shaking her head. "But now look at you, you grown up to be a nice and respectable young man, who makes his living by helping others.

"I tell you, it gives me a chill whenever I see young boys from that hood make something out of themselves. Y'all all turned out to be great. I am very proud of you." Khalon listened patiently watching the seconds on his stainless steel rolex turn into minutes. "You had no mother or father to raise you. In fact, you were even raising your baby sister Aleesa before she passed, may her soul rest in peace.

"God is good; he can turn dirt into gold, yes He can. I'm telling you when I saw that you made officer of the year, I start crying like you were one of my own. It gave me so much joy."

Ms. White eyes almost teared up, but she caught herself so she changed the subject to an even more blessed subject. "You know Kilo is nominated for two Grammys this year? If he wins, this will make four Grammys for him. I make sure I let him know how proud of him I am. You know being around that old devil friend of his could have ended him up in so many different places, you know?"

Ms. White sighed. Leaving for the first time in the conversation, room for Detective Khalon to answer. "Yes ma'am."

"Am sorry baby, why did you come here again, come on in? I just been talking, is it true about what they say? Do we have a burglar on the loose?" Khalon follows Ms. White into the seating room.

"I am not sure Ms. White, but what I have to say you are going to need to sit down for." Ms. White held her head down walking towards the marble top bar that held her children's photos. "Oh my God, just tell me. I don't have time to be sitting down when I get bad news because that's what it sound like it's about to be."

"Kilo is dead," not wanting to keep her guessing any longer. Ms. White walked off, holding her head held high to the ceiling as if she was talking to God right there in her house. "Oh my God, please tell me that this is a joke, please Khalon. I can't take my only boy being gone from me Lord, help me." Ms. White stared off into space for five minutes, then turns to Khalon looking directly in his emerald eyes. "I got God on my side Khalon, and I promised myself if this had ever happened to me, if I had ever lost one of my kids before leaving this world, I wouldn't question his work."

Speaking in her strong voice while fixing her clothes and wiping her tears, she said, "However, I want justice for my son; I want whoever did this to him off the streets. I'm trusting that you would do the right thing and find the one person who is responsible for this."

The detective looked Ms. White directly in the eye as he promised her his word. "You have my word the person responsible for this will pay. You will get justice if I have to miss numerous nights of sleep to do so." Ms. White looked at Khalon with a sense of comfort knowing that he was going to bring justice for her son, the man who had watched him grow himself.

"Ms. White, I do have some questions I would like to ask you if that's okay?"

"It's more than okay baby, but the truth is I'm not sure if I'm going to be any help, because I knew nothing about Kilo's life outside of these walls. That's how he liked it. It gave him comfort and a peace of mind knowing he could come home and not be the artist Kilo but my son Rodger."

Ignoring the fact that Ms. White didn't believe that she could help him, Khalon jumped right into the questioning.

"Is there anyone who would want to hurt him, Ms. White?"

"No, not that I know of, but as I told you before, I don't know much."

"Don't worry I will take the little you gave me and start from there. When was the last time you seen him?"

"Rodgers left my house at 3:30 p.m. yesterday. I had cooked him some cat fish, fried corn, and corn muffins so he came over and ate. Shortly after finishing his food, he left; he told me that he would call me when he got home but he never called. I just figured that he went over to a girl's house or something and forgot."

"Did he seem depressed, stressed, or worried about anything?"

"No Khalon, actually he was very joyful. He was running around here humming to himself like he used to do when he was a boy and had just started liking a girl in school."

"Was there anyone special in his life that he would share his close secrets with?" Ms. White pursed her lips.

"I wish I knew the answer to that."

"Okay, well thank you Ms. White for everything and be damn sure that I'm going to find out who did this to him." Khalon hugged Ms. White tight. "You just worry about getting his funeral together, don't you stress about anything. Give him the burial of a lifetime, his fans would love that."

Ms. White turned Khalon loose nodding her head yes. "I sure will Khalon and I thank you baby, God knows I do; there couldn't be any better person working on this case."

"I will be in touch Ms. White; if I find out anything that I think you should know, I will call you."

Ms. White looked at Khalon while kissing his hand. "Thank you Khalon."

"You don't have to at all Ms. White, not at all," the detective said as he proceeded out the door. Khalon jumped back in his Charger speeding off to the police station. The detective looks at his phone as it vibrated; flashing on the screen was his Captain, he hesitated on picking it up since he knew he was on the way to the station anyway but missing urgent news wasn't a risk he could take. "Yes, Captain Johnson?"

"What's your location, detective?"

"I'm two miles away from the station, is everything okay?"

"Yeah everything is fine. I got someone here who I would love for you to meet."

"If it is a partner, you can keep waiting on me then. I told you once before that I don't work with partners."

"First off, you don't tell me what you do, remember that. Now get down here fast and shut up." The captain hung up leaving Khalon no room for back talk.

"I swear this damn captain is going to make me quit this fucking job." Khalon pulled up to the curve to a stand that sold hot coffee and every magazine you would want to read, from People, New York Times paper, Essence, Vibe, Elle, you name it. On every magazine and paper, Khalon saw Kilo's face. Grammy rapper Kilo killed for speaking out on the Illuminati, Five months after joining the Illuminati, rapper Kilo is found dead, Young, talented, and gone;

Grammy rapper killed for not joining the Illuminati, the media was having a field day with the fact that Kilo rapped about being against Illuminati and although the outside world had no clue about the secret world, they loved to dwell on it. It was a subject that everyone had an opinion on from young people to the elderly, from whites to blacks, to rappers to stock brokers, from the rich to the poor. So anytime the media got a chance to run a story about the Illuminati, they did just that, with a little bit of exaggeration behind it of course.

Since there was no one who was willing to talk about it with the true facts. "Kilo wasn't in no damn Illuminati," Khalon uttered getting out the car and walking up to the stand. Looking at the magazines made him furious. The Illuminati allegedly controlled world affairs and Khalon had known Kilo since he was a boy growing up and being part of any secret organization that had political power and influence on the same people he tried so hard to uplift wasn't in him. He was no Illuminati nominee.

"That will be $7.50, sir," the man that owned the news stand said, interrupting the detective's conversation to himself.

"How much did you say this coffee is?" Khalon said taking a step back, looking at the man a second time.

"You sure are hustling the people, man I tell you?" Khalon jumped back in his Charger and sped off after giving the man his money. He arrived at the police station in less than three minutes. When Khalon entered the doors, everyone's eyes fixated on him. At that moment he knew something was up. A police station full of still officers told him so. Walking towards the captain, he asked, "What's up, captain? Why is everybody staring as if you are giving me a partner from hell?"

The captain quickly snapped, "Would you shut up talking about a damn partner; no one is giving you a partner, at least not at work anyway. Captain pointed at his office window, feeling proud with a grin on his face. Here is the person I want you to meet." Her name is Kelly. She graduated from Harvard. She had seen your picture in the New York Times and she thought you were a cutie. So I figured I would introduce y'all."

Not adjusting to the idea easily, Khalon said, "Come on captain, this is a police station, not a dating service. Besides I told you and the rest of the men in this station that I wasn't looking for any one right now."

"Look I know all that, but all work and no play is not good for you. Now don't be rude, boy. Come in here and speak to the lady. I know no one will ever be able to replace Diana but at least try to have some fun." Enemies turned lovers, Diana was the one women that gave Khalon a mirror to see where his flaws lay. She turned a stubborn man into a very humble one and once he realized the impact she had on him, their love began to make history. Shortly after embracing their love, Diana died of breast cancer, leaving Khalon sour on love.

Khalon looked in the glass window that led to his captain's office, curious to see what the woman looked like. He glanced at the tall caramel skinned lady, who was dressed in a light blue Metro style square neck skirt suit with beige Christian Dior shoes to match. She had shoulder length dreads that were neatly twisted.

Nervously, Kelly twirled in a semi-circle with her hand combing through her dreads as she glanced at the glass the very shy, handsome man watched her through. One look at him and she knew he was the one for her. He stood tall enough for her to wear her

8

good shoes out with and his body was to die for. The sophisticated lady was always attracted to black men with a career and intelligence. She was one of those ladies who couldn't stand the thought of a thug, pants sagging Old Gangster wannabe. Kelly loved the way Khalon's clothes fitted his body perfectly. They weren't too tight or to loose. The detective had on a white button down that complemented his twelve pack with two buttons from the neck unbuttoned showing off just a little of his chest.

Black dress slacks with black Steve Madden shoes completed the attire. Waiting patiently, Kelly thought to herself, Now the only thing he needs is the smell to follow the looks of that body.

Khalon walked in his Captain's office toward the beautiful lady, taking her hand into his. "Hey, how are you?" Khalon asked while kissing Kelly's hand, staring her directly in the eyes.

She was flattered by his gentlemenly ways. "Hey, I'm great and how are you?"

"I'm fine. I apologize for this, its Kelly right?"

"Yes, but you don't have to apologize for anything, it's my pleasure to meet you." Kelly closed her eyes as the two hugged, breathing in the great scent he was wearing, trying her best to exhale softly so he wouldn't hear her, thinking damn this man smells good, there is a God.

Kelly wrapped her hands around his broad shoulders allowing Khalon's hands to hug her thin waist.

"Same here, the only problem is I don't know what they told you to get you here."

"Don't worry, it was nothing embarrassing. Besides like I assured you, it was more of my idea anyhow, I was in a class where your captain was speaking and I helped him with his presentation because his assistant bailed and in return, I asked him to set up a meeting with us. Kelly smiled as if she was shy about her bold move. We can talk about it some more over dinner if you like?"

Khalon paused for a minute, not knowing how to let the lady down easy.

"Don't worry, I know you just recently lost your wife. I will never try to compete or take her place, it's just dinner."

Nodding his head, he agreed, "Okay that will be fine. How about we exchange numbers and I will call you when it is a good time for me?" Khalon took the initiative to set the date up because he knew he had no intentions on making one but politeness was everything.

"Sure, that's a great idea."

After giving the sexy guy her number, Kelly walked out of the captain's office strutting harder than a supermodel. Hoping that detective Khalon was watching her, "I got to get that man. Um, God knows he got me written all over him," Kelly murmured to herself while walking off.

After watching Kelly strut out the building, Khalon had some words for the Captain. "Captain, I advise that you never do that again if you don't want me being accused of hurting some lady's feelings."

Head shaking from side-to-side, mouth semi-wide, and eyes in still formation; the captain was disappointed at the detective's reactions to the beautiful lady.

"You know you are starting to scare me, boy. You sure you like women? Because if you would have introduced me to a black, sexy, educated, and independent woman, I would have been all over her. I would have been the candy to her apple."

Khalon looked at the captain with a serious expression on his face. "Just never do that again, thanks."

"You so damn uptight, boy." Khalon shook his head with a smirk on his face he knew that the captain had good intentions but, he also knew trying to explain to the captain that springing just any girl on him wasn't going to work, his women had to be very rare. "Thank you for caring so much man that means a lot to me, but don't stress yourself trying to find me happiness, you already got all this worry about." Khalon waved his right hand out towards the open crowd of policemen giggling, while patting the captain on the back with his left hand. The two laughed for a second before Khalon walked out of the police station heading to his peaceful and comfortable home. He wasn't rich enough for the Illuminati to get at him and he wasn't too poor where he couldn't enjoy the goodness life had to offer.

Khalon picked up his cell phone that was ringing with an unavailable number on the screen. "Hello."

"Have you thought about my offer or what? I don't have all freaking year for you to answer me," the sexy sounding lady said on the phone.

"First of all, don't be rushing me. Second, don't you ever call me private again. Make your number known so I can know your identity."

"Forget all that. Are you in or what?"

Khalon hesitated before answering. "You sure you have everything we are going to need?" "Yes, I have everything we need."

"Now if we start there is no backing out until the job is done. So if you are just mad for the moment and plan on making up to the man later, then this is not the job for you."

The nameless lady was silent for about two minutes. Thinking twice about her decision, she knew with Khalon backing out wasn't an option.

"Yeah, I know I'm ready," She responded.

"Okay, there are no limits by the way; I know how to find you when I'm ready. We will work on my terms and on my time, for safety reasons and no one, I mean no one should know about this. Do you hear me?"

"Yes." Jarlath: No Point Of Return

Jarlath walked to the kitchen to get himself a cold beverage. When passing the TV in the seating area, he saw the breaking news. "Rapper Kilo shot down in Central Park."

"Lisa!" he called out softly to his maid. "Turn that up for me."

"Yes, sir," the Asian maid dressed in a tight, short fitted black and white maid uniform said while walking to the glass table to get the remote that turned up the 70 inch plasma, which was mounted on the wall.

"Is there anything else you want me to do for you Jarlath?"

"Yes, shut up so I can hear."

The shy, very timid maid walked over to the kitchen to pour Jarlath some nice cold orange juice while thinking, I hope this damn boy is not dead, cause on egg shells I shall walk. The maid knew trouble was around the corner in and out the households if anyone in Jarlath's camp was dead, you just never know what his next move would be and that was scary since every move he made was dangerous.

"The rapper Kilo was found in his car right outside of Central Park this morning. It is said from the officers that the rapper was shot last night around 11:00 P.M," The thin, blonde Caucasian reporter stated on the Channel 5 News.

"Lisa, call Quake Man and tell him I want a meeting set up right now with everyone. Everybody needs to meet me at the office and if I make it there before anyone, there will be a price to pay."

"Yes, sir."

Jarlath walked out of the all-white seating area and headed up the glass spiral stairs that led to his master bedroom. Sitting on the end of his bed, Jarlath dipped his head down in his hands while releasing his tears, watching them hit his light beige mocha Goa rug. Kilo was the first artist Jarlath made famous. He was the best there was when it came to freestyles. Unlike other rappers, Kilo always had a story to tell. He wasn't rapping just to rap. "Know your worth", "The world is ours", & "Knowledge is Power", is music Kilo gave to the black community.

It was Kilo's rapping that inspired Jarlath to start a record label, Black Nation, the most successful hip-hop record label around. Jarlath sat there with the moisture from his tears in his hands while thinking back when he pursued Kilo to become a rapper.

"Thanks for the offer Jarlath but I'm not trying to be no rapper for a living man. It's too much that comes with that territory these days. You got brothers using money for power to prey on the weak and shit. And I will never be down for that shit on a broke day, you feel me?"

"I feel you Kilo, but you have a talent, man; you really need to use it. It will be a shame to see your talent be a waste, just gone down the drain like that. What if I told you that your talent will be only used to empower the weak and to educate the blacks?"

"That would be great, but you can't promise me that. There are some cliques bigger than you who won't allow it."

"You just let me handle them."

"And how the hell you supposed to handle the Illuminati when they come at your ass? I know they done reached you by now as much money you making out here."

"Yeah, I'm well off but nothing like I need to be for them to reach me. However, very soon they will be at me and very soon I will be running the entire Illuminati operation."

"Yo, why would you want to run that shit Jarlath, man? Growing up, I always looked up to you. You was what a brother looked to for inspiration, man, a black entrepreneur on the rise. But you get no respect from me if you join son, I mean no respect son, none whatsoever, you feel me?"

"I hear you but I don't know about feeling you. How do you think I started my damn business? From drug money, another way of killing our people, the same damn people who support my black ass, the same black people who help my business become successful. I sold drugs to their sisters, brothers, sons, daughters, aunts, fathers, uncles."

"Yo Jarlath, but God forgives you. You turned what you did wrong into something positive. You gave back to the communities and shit, you are the reason my sister got a chance in school. You paid for her to go to college and she was no kin of yours. You never asked her for nothing in return but good grades. So how in the hell a man with a heart like that can even think about joining something as cruel as Illuminati? I would expect to hear this from your dog heartless ass friend Ronny but not you."

"Because a man like me knows there are three choices. Stay broke, get down, or get smoked. I'm sure not about to stay broke to stay alive because then what am I living for? To live with limits and not explore the unseen? No one is taking me; I am going to die an old man. So my only choice is to get down and take over the organization for the power is in my hands. I make the calls and you have my word you would never have to be down with the Illuminati. I will make sure of it.

You will be my gift to all the people I fuck over to get to where I'm heading. If they listen to you, they will have the hope. They will have the inspiration that they will receive right along with very good raw music to relate to. Deal?"

"You know what, you a smooth talking, persuading motherfucker Jarlath." Kilo said sitting on his momma's steps watching the traffic pass in Brooklyn. "But to answer your question, yes, if you keep your word, it's a deal."

"My word is all I have as a man, Kilo. You will soon know that." Jarlath stated before dapping Kilo down with a hood anthem hand shake.

Knock, Knock, Knock. The small taps on the door disturbed Jarlath as he was remembering the past. He tried quickly to wipe the tears that were visible on his face before the door opened, knowing that it was prohibited for a man in his position to cry.

"Jarlath, Quake Man said that they are all waiting on you, sir." Lisa looked at Jarlath's face and she knew that he been crying.

"Sir, are you okay?" the maid asked.

"I'm fine, just make sure the next damn time you knock on my door you wait for the go ahead to come in, understood?"

"Yes sir, I understand." Lisa walked over to the tall, handsome, coffee-skinned man, ignoring the fact that she would get fired if she crossed the line in anyway. She sat on the bed next to Jarlath, taking long strokes up and down his back, rubbing softly. "Everyone hurts, no matter what position you are given in life. As a human, no position can be played perfect. I am here if you ever want to talk about anything. I will just listen so you can relieve your stress or clear your thoughts, and of course, everything will be confidential." Lisa kissed Jarlath softly on the earlobe then walked to the closet to gather his

$599,000 black suit made of the finest cashmere, wool and silk, designed by British designer Stuart Hughes, and laid it across the bed. She then took his $1,830 black Berluti shoes and placed them right beside the bed. Jarlath just looked at the maid who never spoke up for herself as she gathered his clothes for the day, thinking to himself, Damn she never speaks or takes up for herself but she gained points today.

"Would you like me to do anything else for you, Jarlath?"

"No, that will be all."

Lisa walked out of the bedroom, running right into Mrs. Rivers. "Hello Ms. Rivers, how are you today?"

"I'm fine. Is my husband in the bedroom?"

"Yes he is."

Alayne walks in getting right to the question she so badly needed an answer to. "Baby, is it true? Is Kilo dead?"

Jarlath looked at his wife and grabbed her, he whispered in her ear, "Yes, Alayne. I am on my way out to see what's going on right now."

Alayne immediately dropped to her knees shaking uncontrollably and cried out, "Who would do this to him, who would want to hurt him?" Hitting Jarlath, she screamed, "He was the only sane person around here! Find who did this to him, and make sure they pay, Jarlath. They must pay, Jarlath."

Jarlath stood firmly while looking Alayne in the eye the entire time. "I never knew you cared so much, wifey."

Alayne stood on her feet, quickly wiped her tears away, and responded, "He was just a good loyal man and it's always hard to lose a loyal friend in this world we live in." Alayne walked away with her head held down, knowing her suspicious husband was wondering why she had just broken down so badly over one of his employees.

Jarlath finished dressing and kissed his grieving wife on her soft pink lips. "I will call you as soon as I know what happened. In the meantime, you are not to go anywhere and I do mean nowhere."

"I can't be locked up in this house, Jarlath. I have a photo shoot to do with Elle Magazine, baby. I can't cancel with them. They will never call me for a shoot again. Not to mention I have to be on the runway tonight."

"Don't worry about Elle, I got them, and you will make it to the runway. Just not alone. I'm coming with you." : Knowing that what he said was final, Jarlath left the room, closing the door behind him with a resounding thud. Alayne crossed her long, skinny legs and sat back on the bed with her immense breasts pushing out of her white tank, and rolled her eyes at Jarlath's cockiness. She was no longer worried about her to; do list because she knew if her husband said he got her, that's exactly what he meant. He never steered her wrong. Alayne turned over on her stomach lying on the bed with her head resting on her forearm. The long Indian Remy weave flowed down her back reaching the dip in her spine. Thinking about how she had made it big in the modeling industry, Alayne's looks and Jarlath's connections equaled to a beautiful, black, successful Victoria Secret Angel.

She met Jarlath in a Brooklyn recreation center. He would often come by to give out money to ambitious young ladies and men who had an interest in going to college. But Alayne was different from the others girls in the Brooklyn recreation center. She didn't have an interest in college. Her interest was becoming famous. She always knew her beauty would take her out of the hood and make her the supermodel she had always dreamed of becoming. All she needed was a little start up. So instead of asking Jarlath for money for college, she asked him for his number, Alayne had dreams that only a man like Jarlath can make happen and needs that only he could please. She knew from the start he was going to be her husband. Jarlath never dated the girls in the recreation center but Alayne was demanding. Jarlath explained to Alayne that his lifestyle did not fit young, black, educated girls because he would just destroy them and that his goal was the complete opposite. He wanted to uplift them and his lifestyle didn't allow it. Alayne ignored that fact and remembered what she desired out of life.

Unable to stop the physical attraction Jarlath had for Alayne, he gave her what she craved… a man in control, success, and a rollercoaster lifestyle. Alayne began to cry thinking about the day she made the biggest mistake on her life, the day she said "I do" to becoming Mrs. Rivers. She had received more than she was bargaining for.

Alayne knew that being famous had its perks, but she didn't know exactly what it was she was getting into, she thought about how she had spent most of her young years with Jarlath. Alayne was thirty years old and she had been with Jarlath for ten years now. There was nothing she had not seen or anything she could not have. A closet full of designers, a diary full of pain, and a passport with many stamps. Alayne's resume was full of experience. From black eyes, to private getaways, to infidelity, to expensive pearls. Jarlath had done everything for her, but love her the way she wanted him to.

"I wonder how suspicious Jarlath got with me crying so much over Kilo?" Pulling her hair, she repeated the words, "Damn, damn! How could I be so stupid?" Alayne's brain wasn't giving her any answer; she didn't know what to do. She felt weak and down to her knees. Alayne began to cry again, recalling the fact that the only man who understood her was killed last night. "Damn you Kilo for leaving me, damn you! How could you do this to me?" Alayne laid down and placed the pillow over her head so that the staff wouldn't hear her crying. She and Kilo had been messing around for five years and Kilo had just proposed to her two weeks prior to him being killed. She said yes and the two were going to tell Jarlath about their relationship, hoping that he would understand it and see it as a way of getting free from Alayne. Alayne never wanted to let go of the throne because she couldn't bare seeing another chic winning. So it was nothing Jarlath could do to get rid of her, but Kilo finally convinced Alayne that money wasn't the only way to success and happiness. Kilo used to comfort Alayne when Jarlath would hurt her by cheating with other woman. The young rapper constantly reminded Alayne that she was worth more than she was receiving. He had even stopped her from trying to kill herself. Now that Kilo was dead, Alayne was starting to feel like she had nothing to live for all over again. The only person who kept her sane was gone and there was no way she was going to be able to survive without him.

Alayne rose to her feet, walking toward the bathroom with tears rolling down her face smearing her mascara and snot running from her nose. Looking in the medicine cabinet, she found the pain pills that her private doctor had prescribed to her for having bad headaches whenever she got stress. Alayne took all the pills and within five minutes she was passed out on the floor.

Twenty-five minutes later, Lisa went to see if Mrs. Rivers needed anything. The five soft knocks on the bedroom door didn't get a response. "Mrs. Rivers, are you in here?" Lisa walked into the bedroom and when she didn't see Alayne, she walked over to the bathroom where the door was cracked opened and pushed it wide opened. To her surprise, Mrs. Rivers was laid out on the floor unconscious. Lisa shook her while repeating, "Mrs. Rivers, Mrs. Rivers, please somebody help me!"

The Rivers' private Chief Kudzu, rushed up the stairs as soon as he heard Lisa's cry for help. Following the trail of Lisa's voice, he found both Lisa and Mrs. Rivers laid out on the floor "What's wrong, Lisa? Oh, my God! What's wrong with her?" Alayne was stretched out on the bathroom floor with an empty bottle of Vanquish pain pills on the his and hers sink.

"I don't know." Lisa said while crying. "Call 911, quick." Kudzu called 911. Right after the call, he began to push down on Alayne chest. "One, two, three, four, five, six, seven. Come on, Alayne hang in there for me. Open your mouth." Kudzu blew his cool, double mint scented breath into Alayne and she began coughing.

"Help is on the way Mrs. Rivers. Just try to stay awake for me baby, please." Kudzu's voice was shaking like a leaf on a tree and his forehead was sweating like he just finished a day's workout. He placed his shaky hands behind Alayne's head so she wouldn't be resting on the floor patiently waiting for the paramedics, hoping they arrived sooner than later. Twenty minutes later the paramedics marched up the spiral stairs, with their black bags in hand. Kudzu's shaky hands and Lisa's dramatic pacing did not affect the two white guys' aura. They remained calm. There was only one reason why supermodel Alayne Rivers was laid out. "We have a thirty year old female suicide attempt, pain killers. Prep ER for pumping of the stomach."

Kudzu met eyes with Lisa and told her, "Call Jarlath and let him know what's going on. I am going to go to the hospital with Mrs. Rivers." Kudzu held onto Alayne while riding in the ambulance with her.

"You are going to be okay, just hold on a little longer for me beautiful, just a little longer." Tears rolled from Alayne's eyes. She heard Kudzu, but she didn't want to, because that meant she was still alive. Kudzu looked at it differently. He felt as if his voice had saved her and that she was thankful he was by her side during that very scary and lonely moment. Less than an hour later, the media pulled up outside the hospital, broadcasting different stories about the supermodel Alayne Rivers.

αααα

Jarlath held a meeting with all of his most important and established employees. That's how he viewed his workers, nothing less, nothing more. He had no friends in the world he was living in. He learned that valuable lesson the hard way with his fame, wealth craving, old friend Ronny. The two were Inseparable for most of their childhood and like any clique they wanted the same thing out of life; a way out of Brooklyn, success and power was the topic of every conversation. The only difference between the two was that Ronny would do anything to get there, even if it meant crossing the ones who loved him most.

Jarlath's clique sat at the long, square table waiting for the first word to exit his mouth like a hungry dog waiting on a bone. "I want to know who is responsible for the heat I am about to receive? Who is responsible for putting a suspension on my money? Who killed my most valuable merchandise?"

21

"Can anyone tell me what happens when my operation is tampered with, and when I have no answers to the problem?"

The silence of the other rappers, producers, singers, and designers surfaced the room.

Jarlath answered his own question. "Yes, that's right. That means some people are going to be losing some sleep tonight. I desire answers and I want them fast. The faster I get my answers, the faster y'all families become safe."

Quake Man shook his head and said, "You will get answers, boss. Be damn sure of that."

"Did I ask you to speak to me, son? I don't remember asking you to speak. All I know, you could have gave me this problem."

"Nawl, Nawl, come on now, Jarlath. Kilo was like my brother. His mother raised me and vice versa. I would be the last person for that job. You got it all twisted."

Jarlath repeated the last of Quake Man's sentence. "I got it twisted. Son, in my world, no one is excused. People will kill their own mother to get what they need. You are no exception. If I'm not mistaken, weren't you the one who just threatened Kilo, your brother's life?"

"Yeah, but I wasn't for real. We argued all the time."

"Listen and hear me well, Mr. Quake Man. You were the last person with beef with Kilo. So as far as I am concerned, you are my number one suspect and if proof don't show up and prove otherwise, there will be some earthquakes for real, Jarlath earth quakes. Now all of you are excused." The entire time Jarlath spoke to his employees, he kept a calm voice about himself. He never raised his voice when he was mad. He never talked when he was angry. Jarlath was a firm believer of letting the anger catch up with the mind so that no stupid mistakes will be made. While talking to the crew Jarlath received a text from Lisa stating that Alayne was taken to the hospital.

He didn't rush to her rescue because he was not surprised. He was well aware of her and Kilo's affair. In fact, he was furious about Alayne putting herself in the hospital because now it was another problem he had to make look good to the media. Jarlath decided not to go to the hospital to see Alayne. Her method for attention was getting old to him. In fact, he was disgusted with the way she was carrying herself as a lady, a wife, and a role model. The extra attention from the media wasn't helping his public image at all and Alayne was well aware of this. As soon as the doctors gave her the clear, he was going to request that she be sent home so that he could give her the talk she was begging for. Jarlath texted Lisa and told her to tell Kudzu to stay with her until she was given the go ahead to be sent home.

Jarlath's security opened the doors swiftly as Jarlath exited the building trying to avoid any media that might have been standing outside of his corporate building in Manhattan. The bodyguards opened the door of the MayBach and Jarlath quickly got into his car. He was so furious about the way that everything was going that all he could do was think about how his life would be if he had kids to go home to. Alayne was never in a rush to have kids because of her career. She believed having a baby would mess up her shape and she was in no good condition to be having that happen. Every day her competition increased because of young girls who had dreams and the ambition of becoming supermodels, especially Victoria Secret Angels.

Jarlath arrived at his cold and lonely mansion. Lisa greeted him at the door. "Hello Jarlath, let me take your coat for you." Lisa took Jarlath's coat while he headed to the bar in the entertainment room.

"Lisa, come turn on this radio for me."

"Yes, sir."

"And quick calling me sir, you make me sound so old."

Twenty-four year old Lisa looked at Jarlath and nodded. "Yes." She sat on the sofa watching Jarlath as he stood at the bar taking three shots of Russian Vodka to the head.

He walked towards Lisa and gave her a demand, wondering if she would obey or not. "Unzip my zipper for me. You said that I could come to you when I needed help, well I do. I need some great head right now." Lisa looked up at Jarlath as he stood in front of her, unzipped his pants, and in no time began sucking his rock hard dick, slurping like he was the popsicle she needed for the hot day in the park. Jarlath took the back of Lisa's head and shoved it towards his dick, not caring that he was choking her. Jarlath heaved his entire dick in Lisa's mouth, fucking her mouth harder and harder while pulling her hair. "Suck it Lisa, choke if you have to, just make this nut come so you can get off my dick."

Obeying Jarlath, Lisa gulped more of his dick into her mouth, hoping that the thought would make him nut. "Aww, now swallow Lisa, like you were craving it all your life." Jarlath wasn't looking for another do as you say girl, Lisa failed the test. For the first time in his life, he wanted a girl who had her own voice, a woman who could stand on her own. A lady who didn't have to have him, but enjoyed having him around. Most of all, he wanted a girl who would give him offspring.

After the great oral, Jarlath walked away, leaving Lisa in the room to clean herself off. The sex only made him yearn more for a rare diamond. Jarlath laid on the sofa, dazing off and daydreaming about having a family that he could come home to after a long day of work. About some kids who would call him Daddy. The life he was adjusted to was becoming a bore. The only thing that stopped him from going off the edge like Alayne was his hope. If he wanted it bad enough, he could get it just like everything else in his life. He just had to get acquainted with his patience.

"Jarlath, do you need anything?" Lisa asked, standing over Jarlath as he lay on the comfortable white sofa.

"No, I'm good. You have given me enough for one night. Sit down, take a break." Lisa sat on the cozy carpet Indian style. Jarlath was curious, he wanted to know if Lisa demanded his commands out of fear, bigger intention like many, or was just into being controlled. "What are your goals? Is there something you want to be in life or you one of them who just flow with the wind? Because I know you don't plan on working for me too long. Most people use me for my recommendations and references. Are you planning on working for me as long as you can?"

Lisa turned to face Jarlath with a puzzled face, she was flattered he asked, but nervous to answer. Lisa didn't want to disappoint Jarlath with her answer. The questions were coming back to back and out of nowhere. "I want to be a news anchor. I think I'm good with talking in front of the cameras. I can pronounce words clearly and I look amazing. I've always desired to do that, but taking care of my five sisters and two brothers kind of put that on hold for me."

"Well you shouldn't let that stop you. I know some people down at Channel Five. I will put in a word for you if you really want to be an anchor lady. Now I'm going to set up the interview and put in a word, but it is up to you to take it to the next level. So, like I tell my employees, put your hustling cap on and go get what belongs to you in life."

Lisa's smile lit up the room. She was totally not expecting Jarlath to help her out with her future. Jarlath couldn't understand it but anytime something was just so wrong in his life the only way he could get a breath of fresh air, was by helping someone with their struggle. It gave him strength to take on his problems. Lisa jumped up and hugged Jarlath, sitting him up on the sofa. "Thank you so much, this means so much to me, thank you."

"It's fine. I wish you luck. If you get the job, I just ask that you will let me know ahead of time. So you can find me another maid. I will also need you to train her as well."

"Okay that's no problem. I can do that. Thank you again, Jarlath."

"You're welcome." Jarlath laid back on the sofa and Lisa left him to his relaxing while she ran to call her sister with the great news.

A SOUTHERN TOWN

The roads were long, dark, and silent. All you could hear was the cool wind that blew the tall aged trees. The scent of fresh cut grass and pine needles covered the air. The houses were distant from one another like a separated couple.

"Maddison, why aren't you sleeping?"

"I can't sleep Zakiya. All I can think about is the carnival and how we going to have so much fun."

"Well if you don't go to sleep, you will never get to see the carnival. Now stop doing all that moving over there. I'm trying to get some rest, little girl."

Because none of momma's Mary Birds were out of the nest yet, they had to share two of the three rooms. The girls were all grown with exception of Maddison, who was only ten, and sharing rooms was becoming a challenge. With three to a room, it was hard to get any sleep, privacy, or piece of mind. The three younger sisters, Layla, Maddison, and Zakiya, shared rooms and the older three Cambria, Harmony, and Melody shared rooms. At the moment, Zakiya was wishing that she had shared a room with the older siblings.

Zakiya tossed and turned, she couldn't sleep. Maddison was keeping her up with the noise and showed no sign of letting up. The sound of soft taps on the window did not help the process. Layla and Zakiya both turned their heads towards the window that sat low to the ground, hoping that the taps were from their boyfriends.

"See who it is, Layla."

"I'm trying to," Layla responded with an attitude. "Oh, it's for you." Zakiya walked over to Maddison's bed, propping her elbow on the windowpane. "Bailey, what are you doing up so late, out here by yourself?"

"I had to see you. Are you going to the carnival tomorrow?"

"Yes, I will be there. Now go home before my mother hears you."

"Ok I'm gone. MUAH!" Bailey laid a fat juicy kiss on Zakiya before leaving, which left Zakiya with a huge smile that reached one ear to the other.

Zakiya went to her bed and laid back down while looking up at the ceiling smiling, humming to herself Rihanna's "Only Girl In The World." Thinking about how much she loved Bailey. Bailey and Zakiya were high school sweethearts. Zakiya closed her eyes thinking about the day when she and Bailey became prom king and queen and the memory made Zakiya smile from ear-to-ear. Zakiya thought to herself it was a reason we were voted most liked couple for the yearbook. Who didn't respect what we have. Every girl in Jackson Town hated the way Bailey, a quarterback, loved Zakiya. Zakiya didn't have to prove herself to anyone. Her popularity came effortlessly but she didn't allow her acceptance get in the way of her school work, being on the dean's list was her proudest accomplishment.

Bailey was Zakiya's one and only and made her stand out from the rest of girls in Jackson Town. Most were on their fourth guy by the beginning of the ninth grade. Zakiya tried to stay grounded and not worry about the girls who threw themselves at Bailey, but it was hard to do sometimes. It would often upset her, but her trust in Bailey kept her calm.

Zakiya fell asleep with Bailey on her mind. The morning was young and bright and today was going to be sweeter than the candy apples she was bound to eat at the carnival. The wind was blowing and the sun was glistening which made the day perfect for the fair, warm by day chilly by night, leaving all the girls who were going to have a boyfriend with them, time to cuddle. Maddison was the first one up in the morning, running down the halls, screaming, "Wake up everybody! Wake up everybody!"

"Maddison, please girl." Harmony screamed out pulling the covers above her large, round breast and over her smooth, dark chocolate face.

"Cambria, I bet you don't know what today is." Maddison peaked her head inside the older girl's room.

"No I don't, so tell me."

"Today is the day I go to the carnival, crazy."

"Maddison, why are you up making all that noise. Dang, people is trying to sleep. You get on my nerves with that." Harmony continued her spat from under the covers. "Leave the girl alone, Harmony. You know she's happy about going to that dang carnival." Cambria expressed while making her twin size bed up.

"That still doesn't give her any reason to be running around here, yelling like she done lost her damn mind." Harmony said before putting the pillow on her head.

"I'm telling Momma on you!" Maddison ran out the room and down the hall, with tears running down her face. The frown on her face would have made a killer heart cave in.

"Who done pissed you off and threw you on the wrong side of the bed this morning?" Cambria said.

"Look, don't start with me today, Cambria. I'm not in the mood."

"I see that, Harmony." Cambria joked.

Melody walked in the room just in time to catch Cambria joke. Melody and Cambria laughed hard, knowing it would only make Harmony that much angrier.

"I swear y'all have nothing better to do, but mess with people early in the morning." Harmony said turning her body towards the wall.

"Girl, shut up, lie down, go back to sleep, and try waking up again with a better attitude." Cambria walked out the room, slamming the door behind her and right behind her was Melody. She reopened the door and slammed it once again.

"Hey Mother, how are you doing on this beautiful Saturday?"

"I'm fine and how are you doing, Ms. Cambria?"

"Oh, I'm fine." Cambria pulled out a chair to sit at the table where their mother, Mary, had pancakes, cheese grits, scrambled eggs, bacon, buttery toast, and nice cold glasses of orange juice waiting for them.

"Momma, this food smells great." Melody said picking up the People Magazine off the bar.

"Well call the rest of your sisters so we can say grace and put that magazine down Melody, eat something before you start reading that garbage."

"Ok Momma. SISTERS COME EAT!"

"Wow! Melody I could have done that." Mary said with a grin on her face, shaking her head side-to-side looking at Melody out the side of her eye, "You a mess girl."

"What Momma? You said to call them, you did not say go get them."

"Well one of your daughters is sleeping and believe me when I say you don't want to wake her up." Melody warned Mary.

Mary shook her head side-to-side once again, with a stale smirk on her face, knowing who Melody was referring to. Layla and Zakiya walked into the kitchen, and pulled themselves up a chair to the eight seat table.

"Zakiya, go get your sister and tell her to come eat now."

"Who you talking about Momma, Harmony?"

"Yes."

"Don't do it Zakiya, don't do it! Zakiya, she's going to kill you!" Melody joked.

The joke was on Harmony once again and the girls all broke out laughing.

"Yawl stop that now."

"Momma, that girl is evil." Layla said crossing her legs at the feet, elbow on the table, hands resting under her chin.

Harmony walked around the bar into the kitchen, surprising the sisters with her appearance. "Yawl tricks always got something to say about somebody when they are not around."

"Watch your mouth in my house, young lady." Mary turned toward Harmony with her right index finger pointing in her direction.

"You didn't say anything to them when they were talking about me." Harmony stated with a confused face and both hands on her hips

"Don't come in here with all that negativity, Harmony. I don't want to hear it." Mary said putting the warm biscuits on the table.

"I will be glad when I can get the heck up out of this house. As soon as Jesse gets back from visiting his family in Ohio, he's going into the Army and we are going to get married and out of this house I go."

"Well congratulations, but until you move, my house, my rules, Ms. Thing. Now sit down." Mary pointed to the chair signaling Harmony to sit down. Mary was an old fashioned Christian woman who believed in marriage before kids, that families should eat at the table together, and that Sundays were the Lord's Day. Hearing Harmony speak about marriage made Mary think of her beloved husband. He was the best and she prayed daily that her girls find the same in there husband Joe Brown. He never hurt her, that's until he died of a heart attack from winning the lottery. Mary was devastated because for one, she didn't believe in gambling and two, Joe promised her he wouldn't gamble. Mary paid for the house and gave the remaining to the church after her mother Annabella begged her not to just give the ticket away since Joe did pay for it with his hard earned cash.

Harmony sat down in her chair continuing her statement. "I swear when I move out of this boring town, I'm never coming back."

"Be careful for what you wish for, Harmony."

"Momma, I'm serious. I dread getting up doing the same thing, nothing to look forward to but the nosey, gossipy people this town has to offer."

"Harmony, be quiet. I have heard enough of your negativity for one day. Bow your heads down so that we can give God thanks for this beautiful breakfast." The girls all bowed their heads and closed their eyes, waiting for their mother to bless their food.

"God, I thank you for providing me with the finances to support my family. I ask that you will bless the food we are about to receive. Amen." Singing like a choir, the girls said Amen right after their mother.

"Momma, when are we going to the carnival?" Maddison said after finally joining the girls. It always took her forever to wash her face and hands and to brush her teeth.

"Whenever your sisters get ready to go Maddison. They will take you with them."

"Momma, I'm not going to be able to watch her because I am going with Bailey," Zakiya said.

"Me neither because I'm going with Harley," Cambria said.

"And I am going with Micah," said Melody.

"And I am going with Troy," Layla jumped from the chair adding her plans quickly. "So are yawl telling me that being with yawl boyfriends is more important than spending time with your little sisters?"

"No Momma, but the carnival is for couples to enjoy time with their soul mates. You know that." Zakiya tried to remind her mother.

Maddison jumped from the table running down the hallway crying to her room.

"Maddison, come back here now. Hope you all are happy." Mary was surprised at her girls' actions and rolled her eyes in disgust

"Yes Momma." Maddison said walking back into the kitchen where Mary was.

"Momma will take you to the carnival, ok."

"YAYYY!"

"Now go pick something out to wear." Muah! Mary kissed on Maddison's cheek who sounded off. Layla wanted to kill the fly in the room. She like the other girls, felt bad and she wanted to clear her conscious so she auctioned Harmony off.

"Momma you should let Harmony take her, she don't have a man."

"Shut up Layla, I do have a man. Key word man, something yawl creeps no nothing about.

Running around here with these scrubs called boyfriends."

Without a second thought Cambria snapped. "And who may you be referring to Harmony?"

"Could be you Cambria, with that railroad track working boyfriend you got? I can see you now being the stay at home mom who hasn't seen the outside of Georgia."

"Girl, I swear you better get out of my eyesight before I catch a murder case." Interrupting and shaking her head Mary said, "I don't understand how y'all argue so much. You are sisters for God's sake." Cambria turned her body towards her momma and said,

"Momma, I swear that girl makes it hard for anyone to love her with that smart mouth she got."

"She got a nerve to look down on someone like she some damn multi-millionaire in the making. I can't wait until your ways blow up in your face. You stuck up, bougie, gold-digger." You could see smoke come out of Cambria's ears she was so upset. Cambria was giving all kind of head rolls, her honey blonde wrap swung effortlessly and you could see the wet in her hazel brown eyes. Lashing out at her sisters always made her emotional.

"Whatever, I'm going to take a nap. Wake me up when the seventies are over with ." Harmony took one last sip of her apple juice before slamming it down on the kitchen table and stormed out twisting every inch of her hips. The sisters watched as Harmony strut out; collectively they shook their heads side-to-side showing disgust on their face. For five seconds you could hear the seconds on the mounted wall clock tick. Zakiya broke the silence with a lighter conversation.

"Layla, can I borrow your autumn colored scarf?"

Layla looked at Zakiya confused, raising her left eye briefly. "Why would you want to wear that old thang?"

Zakiya twirled around in a circle and out the kitchen while saying, "Because honey, I can make anything look good."

"Well help yourself Ms. Lady, but I just can't see you turning that scarf into fashion. It is so yesterday."

"You just let me worry about that." Zakiya said walking down the hallway to her room. Without thinking she knew exactly what to put on with the sweater to bring its best features out, so she reached in one of the two dressers that belonged to her and pulled out her favorites.

Zakiya slid on her flesh tan leggings that matched the color of her skin, threw on her orange-red sweater to keep warm in the late night cool, brown leather fashion cow girl boots for spice, and the autumn multi-colored scarf to top it off. Zakiya's hair was styled in tight pin curls that hung past her shoulders. Fully dressed, Zakiya was ready to hit the scene and be seen.

"Well I'm gone yawl. I will see yawl at the carnival." She shouted out in the hallway on her way out the door.

"Where you out to?" Melody said coming out the bathroom with Ambi even and clear exfoliating wash on her face.

"I am going to Eva's house." Zakiya walked out the room, skipping down the hall and out the door. Eva lived only a couple blocks away from Zakiya and it took no time for Zakiya to get there. Zakiya began knocking on the door, while looking around to see if Eva was outside.

"Who is it?"

"It's me, Eva. Open the door."

Eva rushed down the thirteen stairs to the door and the end at the last step you could hear her breathing slightly heavy but she didn't show it, you only seen white teethes as she smile, happy to see her friend at the door. "Hey girl, come in."

"Why aren't you dressed at this hour of the day?" Zakiya said taking a look at Eva pink and yellow girl's rock pajamas.

"I'm putting on my clothes now. Come on upstairs to my room." Eva took the lead and ran up the stairs before following her. Zakiya spoke to Eva's momma who was sitting propped up in the living room watching days of our lives.

"Hey, Ms. Jackson."

Eva's momma glanced at Zakiya and responded in slow motion. "Hello." It wasn't a where you been, I have not seen you expression on Ms. Jackson's face; her house was like Zakiya's second home. Almost daily Zakiya came over to Eva's house. As soon as the girls enter Eva's room, Eva asked.

"Kiya, you are going to the carnival, right?"

"I'm not sure if I will." Zakiya said taking a seat on the end of Eva's full sized bed.

"What?" Eva turned from the closet where she was standing with her hand on her hip and eyes big all ready to be disappointed.

"I was just playing girl. Yeah I'm going. You know any time this town gets a little excitement the whole town go crazy."

"So is your booksy going with you?"

"You know it. He came over last night tapping on the window asking me if I was coming with him, as if I had plans on going without him. Anyway, where is your boo thang and is he coming with you?"

"No we give each other space, something you and Bailey know nothing about."

"We do give each other space. If I give him anymore space, he'll float right into one of these groupie bitches' arms." Zakiya turned on her stomach stretching out on Eva's bed with her feet hanging off the end, watching Eva switch into gear for the day.

"True, because every chick in Jackson wants Bailey." Eva said turning from the dresser mirror she stood in front of to get dressed.

"Well I guess I just have to go by myself this year." Eva pouted, with her lip poked out.

"Why aren't you and Ryan going to the carnival together? And don't give me that we need our space crap this time."

"Well the truth is Ryan and I broke up. We have been apart for about two weeks now."

"Why didn't you tell me Eva?"

"Because I hate the fact that my relationships never work out. I'm not like you. I'm on my fourth boyfriend and you haven't even left the first one yet."

"Awwl come here baby, I had no idea." Zakiya jumped up from the bed with her arms out walking toward Eva with them wide open.

"Well it's his loss, not yours and you coming to the carnival with me." Zakiya said while hugging Eva tight.

"I don't want to be no third wheel." Eva pushed away from Zakiya with a smirk on her face.

"I don't want to hear it honey, now come on get your things so we can go." Zakiya demanded.

Once Eva finished dressing, she and Zakiya walked to the carnival which was only two blocks away from Eva's house. Zakiya never got an answer on the reason Eva and Ryan went their separate ways, so she brought back the topic.

"So what happened with you and Ryan?"

"He is not on my level. It's like we on two different pages you know?"

"Yeah I feel what you saying, but you're still not telling me what happened."

"Well first off, I asked Ryan what he wanted to do with his life and he responded, 'Shit, I'm flowing with the wind right now.' I don't know Zakiya. I think he just plans on living off his momma all his life and I can't have that kind of laziness for a man. Then a girl called his phone while we were together."

"Oh hell nawl." Disgusted, Zakiya tooted her nose and shook her head no. To her that behavior was not accepted.

"That's what I'm saying, that's some disrespectful shit. Agreeing to Zakiya's low tolerance attitude, Eva nodded her head yes. Then every time we're together he got some chick calling his name like he some damn celebrity or some shit. You already broke with no ambition and then you want to be cheating on top of that shit."

"Yeah, I feel you on that friend. Well you know what I say. We're young, sexy, with a bright future ahead of us so one bus don't stop no show"

The girls laughed.

"You crazy Zakiya."

THE BIG WIN

Zakiya and Eva walked down the long dirt road that led them to the carnival, the rocks crunched loudly under their feet.

"I don't understand why they don't put some houses on these streets, then maybe it wouldn't seem so long and boring," Eva said curious.

"Eva, that's why they call this the country, girl."

"If you go to Atlanta, you will see the streets filled with houses, small convenient stores, and retail stores." Zakiya said responded.

"Now wait a minute we got a downtown too."

"Girl, that's barely a downtown. I bet you haven't even been outside of Jackson, have you?"

"Yes I have. My momma and I go to the mall in Atlanta all the time."

"Yeah when it's the holidays, us country folks gather up and take what we call a road trip to Atlanta."

The two laughed at Zakiya's joke about their town.

"Well, I think it is a crying shame most of these people here have spent their entire life staying inside of this circle called a town." Zakiya said holding her arms out toward the town.

"Well it wouldn't be that bad if they just added some things in these empty areas."

"That would never happen."

"Do you want to know why they wont add any houses or buildings in this area, because then where will the grass grow, or the horses who like shitting up the grass, where will they go?"

"Yea I guess you right. If peoples only knew how we mess with them damn animals, they wouldn't want their animals down here anymore."

"True, but I never mess with them. Shit, I barely want to get close to them. I hate that smell."

"Well you eat them. Besides your man Bailey is one of the ones who used to get a kick out of messing with them dang animals when we were in school. He couldn't miss a day, without hearing them MOO!" He got a kick out of torturing those animals. Zakiya covered her mouth trying not to laugh so loud at Eva's imitation of the cows walking toward the town's nameless gas station.

"Oh hell nawl trick, you sounded just like that damn cow. Look, I need to go inside of the gas station before we get to the fair."

"Why? We can eat when we get there. Shoot that's the best part about going!"

"I know. I'm not about to get anything to eat. I need to play my numbers."

"You do realize how old you sound, right?" Eva and Zakiya giggled at the fact. "You sound like Trisha's momma down there by the tracks, always got to play their numbers."

"Girl, these numbers are going to be my tickets up out of this shameful town one day. You know Trisha's momma hit big, I just don't understand why she still here."

"Zakiya your mother would have a heart attack if she knew you were playing numbers."

"I know that's why you are going to keep your mouth shut." Zakiya stated pointing her right index finger at Eva. You can hear the rocks and dirt from the paved roads crunch while the girls walked in the isolated store.

"What can I do for you today Ms. Zakiya?" The white man with raggedy teeth and tobacco in his mouth asked Zakiya.

"Well you can give me three of them Jumbos and I want to play the cash three and the fantasy five."

"Zakiya your mother would kill me if she found out I was letting you play the numbers."

"Well it isn't much she could do now is it Bob, now that I'm grown in all." Eva burst out laughing at Zakiya mocking the man who had been running the store since they were born. Zakiya continued with her sassiness.

"I am grown now Bob and I have the right to play whatever I want, so if you would please be so kind and play these numbers before they come out. Thank you."

Bob looked at Zakiya and shook his head side-to-side. "Girl you are demanding just like your mother." Bob said while waiting on Zakiya's receipt to print out. "Well here is your numbers and your receipt."

"Thank you, Bob."

"Where yawl girls heading, to the carnival?"

"Yep you know it." Zakiya said picking her tickets up off the counter.

"All right, have fun." Bob waved the girls off.

"We will." Zakiya looked down at her tickets making sure that Bob got her numbers right. "I cannot believe you just spent all that money on some damn tickets." Eva said rolling her plum-colored contacts.

"Yep, I am hoping to get all that money back and some."

"So did you win anything off your scratch offs?" Eva said after Zakiya put her penny in her back pocket and threw the tickets on the ground.

"Nope, but I'm not worried about it, one day I will."

Eva shook her head as they continued on up the road. "I know your mother is a Christian and all and she believes in nothing but the right doing and sometimes I even think she is crazy for being so giving, but I'm with her on this one about buying those tickets. It's a waste of time. Only so many people win and the odds of them people being from a small county like Jackson are very slim to none."

"That's where you are wrong. The most wins have come from the country people." After five minutes the girls were close enough to the fair to see it.

"You smell that Zakiya?"

"What?"

"The good smell of funnel cakes, polar sausages, and nachos, baby."

"Oh yeah, I smell it."

"Are your sisters coming?"

"Yeah they're coming."

"Have you talked to Bailey?"

"He'll just meet me at the fair. You know him, he got to get some boy time in."

"Don't they all. I know Maddison must be so excited."

Zakiya looks at Eva and poked her lips out and rolling her eyes. "Girl is she. That child got on my nerves last night with all that damn anxiousness. She couldn't even go to sleep, tossing and turning back and forth. I had to threaten her by telling her if she didn't go to sleep that she wasn't going to go."

"Why you do her like that? You know how we used to be when we were her age. So anxious we watched the sunrise. It must be fun having a lot of sisters in the house."

"NOPE!"

"You say that, but I promise you having a house of sisters is far better than having a house full of brothers."

"At least you know it's all about you, Eva. You're the only girl, so everything favors your way."

"Yeah, but I had no one to play with. That's why I am always at your house 24/7."

"I guess you're right, I just can't see it. Yawl get to wear each other's clothes, talk about other girls, and most of all, tell each other secrets."

"Hold up for minute, hold up," Zakiya said searching through her Russet suede fringe shoulder bag for her vibrating phone.

Zakiya searched blindly for a long five seconds rushing, trying to catch the phone before it quit ringing but because of the junkie purse she couldn't. "Dang now it has stopped."

"You should clean that junkie damn purse out." Eva snapped

The phone began vibrating again and the girls stopped walking; the noise from the cars passing made it hard for Zakiya to hear the phone.

"Whoever it is they want to talk to you bad," Eva opened Zakiya purse wide joining the search.

"It's probably my momma, here it is. Hello." Zakiya held the phone to her ear with her shoulders using her free hands to put her lottery tickets and receipts back in her bag.

"Hey, where are you?"

"I'm about to walk in the fair. Where are you?"

"Um, outside your door," Eva could hear a voice through Zakiya's phone but she couldn't make out the gender or conversation.

"Oh baby, I'm sorry. I meant to tell you to just meet me at the fair." Zakiya voice softened up.

"Never mind that, your momma got the ambulance outside her door; you might want to get here. I heard your sisters crying, but I'm not sure why. When I asked Harmony what happened she cursed me out and said mind my own damn business."

"Oh my God, ok baby thank you for telling me. I'm on the way." Zakiya voice went from soft to dramatic in seconds.

Eva stared at Zakiya the whole time, anxious to see what was being said over the phone. "Who was that? What did they say?" "That was Bailey; he said that the ambulance was at my momma's house and that my sisters were crying."

"Oh my God, come on, we got to go."

Zakiya and Eva quickly walked down the dirt road heading back to Zakiya's house. They quickly discovered that fast walking wasn't getting them there fast enough so they began to run.

Zakiya was running and praying to God all at once. "Please God, let my mother be ok."

Eva was out of breath yet she still responded to Zakiya's prayer. "She will be, don't worry."

"Shit this is why I told my momma to get me a car. I am too old to be walking." Eva spitted out trying to catch her breath.

Zakiya ignored Eva and ran faster. After all the running, Eva and Zakiya finally made it. Eva bent down, holding her knees, trying to catch her breath, breathing heavily while standing in the front yard of Zakiya's house.

Zakiya never stopped, running into the house. Harmony was the first one Zakiya saw standing in the kitchen over the sink, washing her hands. "Where is Momma?" Zakiya asked while trying to catch her breath.

"What you all out of breath for honey? You must have ran here!"

Zakiya snapped back, "Yes Harmony, now where is Momma?"

"Oh that bomb boyfriend of yours must have told you with his nosey ass."

"Are you serious right now, like for real, are you serious right now?"

Although Harmony came off as a bitch to Zakiya, she was only trying to avoid the question that was thrown at her repeatedly from her baby sister and she didn't want her big mouth boyfriend to scare her. She didn't know how to tell her younger sister that their mother had a heart attack, especially since their father died from a heart attack. Harmony sipped her sweet tea and responded calmly.

"She just had a heart attack, she will be fine."

"A heart attack? How could you sit here and say just a heart attack she'll be fine. You know you really are a cold hearted BITCH!" Zakiya ran out the kitchen into the living room where she sat on the sofa, bowing her head in her hands as she rested her elbows on her knees, crying her heart out. All she could hear was the TV and the beats from her heart, "1, 0, and 4. There you have it, the cash three for today.

The pot was extremely high today so for my cash three winners, you will be taking home 85,000." Zakiya looked up as she had seen her number on the TV. She was in disbelief.

Eva stormed in on Zakiya's teary face staring at the TV. "You ok girl? Harmony told me what happened."

"Yeah I'm fine; all I can do is pray to God right now because he holds all the cards."

"True. Why are staring at the TV, Zakiya, like you just seen a ghost?" Zakiya was in a daze. All Zakiya could think about was her father and mother. Her father won the lottery and he died. Now she had won the lottery and she was praying that didn't mean her mother was going to have to die because of it. Zakiya knew that she would never be able to live with herself if it happened that way, it was a bittersweet situation. Meanwhile in the kitchen; Harmony wiped the tears that started to form on her face and swallowed her pride, walking out the kitchen into the living room. "Are you ok, baby sister?" Harmony tilts her head to the side poking her full heart shape lips out.

"Yes, I'm fine Harmony." Zakiya said turning her attention to Harmony

"I just didn't know how to tell you that she had a heart attack, please forgive me."

Harmony walked over to the sofa with her arms out to give Zakiya a hug.

"I forgive you." After hugging Harmony set on the sofa as they continue the conversation.

"So Cambria went to the hospital with momma?" Zakiya asked

"Yeah, I am waiting on them to call me now.

Harmony turned to the back wall and looked at the clock. I couldn't leave because Maddison is in the back taking a nap, plus we didn't want her to go down there anyway."

"Yeah, she would be asking all kinds of question and stuff. Zakiya said shaking her head agreeing to Harmony decision.

"Well I'm about to get dinner started." Harmony said after popping up from the sofa.

"Do you need me to help you, Harmony?"

"You can if you feel like it."

"Yeah, sure."

Eva walked in the kitchen with Zakiya and Harmony. She loved their bond and being around them made her feel like she had sisters. Harmony had the leg quarters in the sink being ready to get seasoned and dropped in the grease she had warming up on the stove. Zakiya took out the corn on the cob. While she was taking out the corn, Eva took a boiler out and filled it up with water, placing it on the stove.

"Eva, you know you don't know anything about cooking, honey." Harmony said shaking her head.

"Girl, I know that corn's supposed to be boiled." Harmony and Zakiya laughed at Eva but she didn't mind as long as it took their mind off their mother, even if it was for a quick second. While laughing, Eva secretly prayed that God placed a blessing hand down on Ms. Mary, she knew the girls wouldn't be able to take losing her too.

Zakiya, Harmony, and Eva all turned their heads towards the door when they heard the door open. "Who is that?" Harmony said with a high pitch voice.

"It's us," Cambria said.

"Oh, so what's going on with Momma, is she ok?" Zakiya didn't let the girls get in the house good before she asked.

"Why y'all leave her down there by herself anyway?" Harmony added to the list of questions?

"Momma is fine; it was just a mild heart attack. The doctors said that she would just have to start taking it easy. Momma told me to bring Melody and Layla home and start dinner because we all knew who was left here in charge." Cambria the oldest sister said.

"Yeah and don't yawl all feel stupid. I already got dinner started."

"Yeah, I see and I am very proud of you Harmony, you growing up; now move to the side because we all know you don't know what you doing with this chicken." Cambria said joking hitting Harmony hips with hers, taking over seasoning the chicken.

All the girls started laughing.

"Eva, you staying over for dinner?" Layla asked.

"Yeah, I'm staying; I haven't been in this kitchen cooking for nothing."

The girls laugh even harder. The noise carried down the halls and into Mary's room where Maddison was sleeping. Maddison was eager to see what the laugher was about so she got up stretching, following the noise in the kitchen. She walked right in pulling a chair at the table next to Layla.

"Girl you put a pot of water on and now you think you Chef Eva."

"Yep, that took a lot of work to do Layla," Eva replied while the girls continued to laugh around the kitchen table.

Zakiya took a good look at the girls joking around before walking out the kitchen, looking up toward the ceiling, thanking God for letting their mother be ok. She didn't want to tell anyone that she won the lottery so Zakiya went to her room to hide the tickets under her mattress. "I will handle that situation tomorrow. Today, I'm just going to be thankful for my mother's well-being."

"Zakiya what you doing back there, don't be trying to get out of cooking." Melody said stepping out the kitchen to peek down the hallway.

"I'm using the restroom, honey I'll be back. I know yawl love my cooking."

Zakiya rushes back out the room heading to the kitchen. She didn't want them to get too suspicious. "I hope y'all haven't burnt the biscuits because last time Melody burned them."

"Awwl that was a mistake, stop bringing up the old days." The girls start chuckling.

They were laughing about almost everything, feeling relief about their mother's well-being.

"Who saying the grace because GOD knows we need one." Zakiya asked pulling her chair out at the table to seat.

I'll say it and I guess I will just spend the night over as well. Maddison get out the pantry and come join us," Eva said.

"You know you wanted to stay over anyway." Harmony added.

"Of course, yawl my sisters," Eva bowed her head to begin grace and the girls did the same holding each other's hands. "God, I ask if you will please bless the hands that prepared this meal and God I ask if you would please put a blessing hand on my mother. In Jesus name we pray AMEN."

"AMEN."

"Thanks Cambria."

BETRAYAL

The old school, slow music bumping from the Kawasaki radio system was relaxing and soothing to Tiffany's guests. She was having the best sleep over going away party yet. All of her close friends from high school and the entire football team came over to her sister's new apartment. Tiffany's older sister, Rhonda, was gone for the weekend and Tiffany was celebrating her acceptance to Alabama State University, standing as tall as a stallion with long, brown legs and curvy hips. You couldn't find a flaw on Tiffany if you had a magnifying glass.

Her hair weave was done so neatly people often mistake it as her real hair, which wasn't so short itself. Her breasts were a full C cup and they stood firmly. Tiffany's Chanel dress hugged her hips, as she twisted past the boy she always wanted. Tiffany could feel Bailey eyes watching her, so she doubled back stopping in front of him.

"So when do you go off to school?" Tiffany asked Bailey starting off the conversation.

"I'm leaving at the end of July so I can get everything situated before school starts. Plus I want to learn my surroundings a little early."

"When are you leaving?"

Tiffany looked around, twirling her hair and poking her boobs out toward his chest. "Around the same time," she answered. "I'm just waiting on my mother to get my Bentley before I leave."

"Your mother is getting you a Bentley for graduating?"

"Yeah, I already got it. I just got to wait for it to finish getting painted. The original color was black but I wanted it red, so my momma had it painted for me. Would you like to see some pictures of it? I got some in my bedroom."

Bailey looked around at the room full of people, looking to see if anyone was watching him and Tiffany talk. Bailey recognized the game Tiffany was running, but it didn't stop him from entertaining her. Plus, he really wanted to see how her car looked. "Yeah, you can show me."

Tiffany blinked her eyes twice and swung her hair in circular a motion as she walked off, signaling for Bailey to follow her.

Bailey's conscience was messing with him. His eyes were wide and his heart was beating, you would think the people at the party could hear his heart. He looked so paranoid as he slowly walked down the hall that led to Tiffany's sister's guest room.

"Come in, you act like somebody is going to bite you."

"So where is the picture?"

"If you come in I will show you. Dang, you paranoid like a drug dealer."

Bailey came in and shut the door softly so that none of their friends would hear them in the back room. He had hoped that none of them realized they were missing from the party. Bailey sat on the queen size bed looking at Tiffany put the R. Kelly CD in the Sonic radio.

The music was set at a low tone, setting a relaxing mood.

"So what's the deal with you and Zakiya?"

"What you mean? She my girl."

"But for how long? You go off to Alabama in a couple of weeks, how do yawl really think yawl going to keep a relationship like that?"

"How you know she's not coming to Alabama as well?" Bailey said trying to convince himself that he was faithful to his girl.

"Because I know her Christian mother and she will never let her go away to school, she is going to want her baby to go somewhere right here in Georgia." Tiffany eased closer to Bailey.

"Why, what's up, why you asking me all these damn questions about my girl anyway?" Bailey took the pillow and tucked it behind his head before lying down.

"Because her time is up, it's my turn now."

Bailey just looked at Tiffany admiring her boldness. "Girl, you are crazy."

"No boy, I'm for real." Tiffany walked over to Bailey and grabbed his face as she kissed him on his cheeks twice then slid her tongue over to his lips.

Bailey's dick began to grow hard. He so badly wanted to tell her to stop, but his body was craving it. It had been over two months since Zakiya gave him some and he knew she wasn't planning on giving him any time soon. But, his heart was telling him to be considerate of the girl he loved, knowing she would be completely embarrassed if the news got out in the small town. "Nawl come on stop! What you think you doing?"

"Something your girl has not been doing right," Tiffany replied quickly, taking her hands and unzipping Bailey pants, knowing that he wasn't going to stop her. As soon as Tiffany unzipped his pants, Bailey's hard dick popped up leaving Tiffany to do what she wanted to do for a long time.

"Which one would you prefer, head," Tiffany kisses Baileys hard dick, "a good ride," She then turns her round ass toward Bailey man hood and push up on it leaving the arch of her ass in the air. "Or both?" Tiffany stood up between Bailey opened legs with both her breast in her hands kissing them softly with every peck sounding off.

Bailey was no longer saying no. He massaged his balls and said "Both." Tiffany slowly bent down on her knees in front of Bailey, resting both hands on his knee caps.

She took a mouth full of Bailey's dick slurping until he came in her mouth. When she was done with option one, she decided to dance for him off R. Kelly's hit song "Feeling on your Booty." Feeling herself, Tiffany slowly slid the Chanel dress off her curvy body. The admiration in Bailey eyes gave her all the confidence she needed to get it popping, literally. Tiffany turned facing the wall so her ass could applaud Bailey for being a man. Every clap sounded off, you could hear her ass clapping over R Kelly hits. Any move Bailey could dream of a stripper doing Tiffany was bringing to reality; from p-popping to splits. After the intense dance, Bailey's dick was hard again and he was ready to fuck her like a mad man.

Bailey stood up pulling Tiffany to him biting on her neck while grabbing a hand full of ass. After losing his patience, Bailey threw Tiffany down on the bed and pushed her legs back toward her ears. Bailey spit on Tiffany's clitoris before shoving every inch of his hard steel down her hole. You could hear the sound of his balls slapping her vagina as he went in and deep, out and hard, Tiffany was screaming so loud the whole party heard her but that didn't stop Bailey. He had no worries, he fucked her not caring an ounce if he was hurting her.

After twenty long minutes, Bailey took his smooth, chocolate wet dick out of Tiffany's vagina and shoved it down her throat making her catch every drip of his warm nut. Tiffany was choking and gagging but Bailey didn't care. He took his hands and gripped the back of her head, pushing it further down onto his penis. Bailey was quiet the entire time but the moment his nut was released, he growled louder than a lion. He snatched Tiffany away from his dick by her hair and laid on the bed, watching as she went into the full bathroom. Tiffany washed up and slid on the sexiest pajamas she packed.

"I'm just going to tell everybody that the party is over and that my sister is on the way. That way we can have the rest of the weekend to ourselves." Bailey shook his head, closing his eyes while his dick hung free covered in cum. The guests were already packing their things after hearing Bailey and Tiffany fuck so loudly in the room, so Tiffany didn't have to say much. She just locked the door after her friends and walked back to the room feeling like a million dollars. The smile on her face was priceless.

Three weeks of planning and it was finally paying off. Tiffany had just accomplished what she set out to do three weeks ago. She only applied to Alabama State University because she knew Bailey received a full scholarship there for football and the party was only a party to get Bailey in her bed. Tiffany walked in the room, standing in the door watching as Bailey slept. She then walked softly towards him crawling on the bed.

"Baby are you thirsty, do you need anything?" Tiffany whispered in Bailey's ear while rubbing her hands up his chest.

"No, just clean my dick, lay down and rest up for round three."

"Yes baby anything you need. Muah!" Tiffany kissed Bailey on the cheek then walked into the bathroom, fetching a warm rag so that she could respect his wishes. Gently, she washed his dick off with the rag, kissing it from the top of the head to his jingling balls. She couldn't help herself; she took his balls and gulped them in her mouth, licking and kissing all on them.

When she finished, she cuddled up in his arms, laid on his chest and listened to his heartbeat. After five minutes, she lifted her head back up to kiss and suck on his neck hoping that Zakiya would see the hickies. "Goodnight baby, I love you."

αααα

Zakiya woke up early on Monday morning. She couldn't sleep, tossing and turning all night. For the first time in a long time, she couldn't wait for the morning to reach her. Today she gets her money wired to the bank from hitting the lottery. God had answered all of her prayers. Her mother was well, so she no longer feared losing her momma for the sake of winning the lottery. She had a good man and now she was blessed with the money to help start her career, whatever that might be.

"Zakiya, why you up so early all dressed and everything?" Layla asked.

"I got to go meet Eva for something. Go back to sleep Layla and quit being nosey." Zakiya walked out of the house swiftly trying not to wake up anyone, especially her nosey Christian mother.

Skipping through town like she was the only girl in the world, Zakiya stopped at Bob's gas station to play her numbers on her way to Sun Trust.

"Hey there girl, what you doing up so early?"

"Oh. I needed to take care of some business this morning Bob."

"So what you going to do with all that money?" "I saw your numbers fall."

Zakiya gave Bob a questioning look with her forehead wrinkle and left eye brow raised.

"Now Bob, don't you be going around blabbing your big mouth to everybody in town about that money."

"Oh I know better than that. I was hoping that you didn't." Bob was hoping Zakiya didn't run her mouth to her friends about having money, money caused problems and he knew a lot of money with no plan would turn into no money in no time.

"No of course not, well that's good you better keep it that way."

"Hey, Zakiya."

Zakiya turned to the door where the nice built muscular basketball player from school was standing. "Oh hey Robert, what's up with you?"

"Oh nothing. Have you seen your big head friend Bailey?

"I haven't heard from him all weekend."

"Oh, I take it you haven't heard then."

"Heard what Robert?" Zakiya heart dropped to her knees, for some strange reason she felt the news wasn't going to be good. Her palms were sweaty and she couldn't stop her thoughts. They were running through her head faster than Robert could get the message out. What could Robert possibly say to me that would be beneficiary? "I hate to be the one to tell you, but I thought the town would have told you by now."

"Told me what Robert?"

"Bailey was at Tiffany's sister's apartment with her. She had a going away party for her getting accepted to the same school Bailey's going to."

Zakiya cut Robert off, completing his sentence, "Alabama State University."

"Yeah, that one. Anyway, they went in the bedroom while the party was still going and just started fucking." Robert said his last word in a low tone while he picked invisible lint off his white V-neck t-shirt, he couldn't look Zakiya in her eyes when he told her the disturbing news. "Everybody heard them and once they finished, Tiffany put everybody out and went back in the room and laid up with the nigga from what I hear."

Zakiya tried to fight back her tears. The last thing she needed was Robert going back and telling Bailey that she was crying. "Oh that's good for them, we was breaking up anyway."

"Oh for real Zakiya, I didn't know yawl was going through things. Yawl always seemed like the perfect couple to me. That's probably why that nigga did that then, to get back at you, knowing damn well somebody was going to tell you because I know my boy would have never disrespected you like that if yawl wasn't mad at each other." Robert rubbed his deep waves with his right hand while his left hand remained tucked in his grey sweat pants. "Don't even sweat it or let it get to you and please don't tell that nigga I was the one who told you."

"Oh I won't. Trust me Robert, and you right I won't let it stress me, period. I am too blessed to be stressed." Zakiya eyes and head began rolling without intention while her hands rested on her hips.

"That's what's up."

"All right, I will see you around." Robert decided not to play his momma's numbers and walked out the store. The tension between him and Zakiya was somewhat weird and uncomfortable. He was dying to get out the store.

"Ok Robert, bye." Tears started to roll down Zakiya's face. She quickly wiped them as she turned to Bob to pay him for the snacks she just picked up. Bob saw that the girl was hurt so he took it upon himself to remind her of the blessing she just recently talked about having. "Hey you, hold your head up. It was bound to happen. Yawl both young with a future ahead but the only difference is yours is brighter. Now go get that money and do what you always planned to do. Get the hell out of this small town and explore."

Zakiya looked up at Bob with a cracked smile on her face and said, "Thank you Bob. I needed that."

"Anytime beautiful."

Zakiya rushed out the store running and before she could even let her tears drop from the pain of Bailey's betrayal, she was at Tiffany's sister's door beating it down.

"Who is it?"

Zakiya ignored the question and continued to beat the door down.

"Alright, alright, I'm coming." Rhonda opened the door and the frustration on Zakiya face greeted her.

"Yes, may I help you?"

"Where is that whore sister of yours?"

"Excuse me?"

"You heard me where is that bitch?"

"Who is that at the door?" Tiffany asked, coming around the corner.

"Some girl who's looking for you obviously."

Not surprised at all, Tiffany spoke to Zakiya in a calm bitchy tone, "Oh hey, what took you so long to come?"

"Bitch I could strangle you right now," Without a sight of red, Zakiya's hazel eyes read danger.

"Go ahead and I will make it my business to press charges." Tiffany crossed her arms and rested them on her bust while standing back on her legs.

Rhonda turned to Tiffany, asking her "What the hell is going on?"

"Why don't you tell your sister what you were doing in her apartment while she was away this weekend?"

"Tiffany, what the hell did you do in my apartment while I was gone? Did you have a boy in here?" Rhonda turned to Tiffany giving her eye-to-eye with a curious face.

"She had more than a boy; she had a whole damn football team in here. Why she was in your bedroom fucking one of them, letting the others hear her scream."

"WHAT!" Rhonda shouted, turning back to Zakiya shaking her head with wrinkles in her forehead and nose touted up. "She couldn't have because her and her boyfriend was here all weekend baby, so I don't know what you heard from the streets out there but it's a lie." Rhonda tried her hardest to convince herself because the truth was just too hard to swallow. "The girls around are here always telling lies and making up rumors about Tiffany because she is beautiful. Now get the hell away from my door."

Zakiya snapped back at Rhonda quickly, "Her boyfriend? That bitch was here sleeping with my fucking man."

Rhonda turned around to Bailey who was hiding in the kitchen. "Did you or did you not spend time with Tiffany the whole time I was gone?"

Zakiya busted open the door. Zakiya strained her eyes and stared for a minute before she said, "You been here the entire time and you never said anything?

So is this who you with? You couldn't be man enough to tell me that it was over Bailey?"

Bailey cuts Zakiya off, answering the most important question.

"No I'm not with her. I fucked up and I will admit to that but I don't want her, never did. She was a fuck and that's all and even if you leave me, I won't be with her. She will never compare to you baby. You are the only girl I have ever loved. I just let my dick and young ways get in the way of that and I will never do that again, you have my word."

Zakiya had more tears running down her face then a rainy day in Florida while Tiffany looked at Bailey as if her heart had been torn away from her. "What do you mean I was just a fuck?" she finally asked. "I told you I love you Bailey and I meant that."

"Tiffany I never loved you and I never will, so get over it alright." Bailey's face looked harder than a red brick.

The reality of Bailey's drama hit Zakiya in the face and she stormed out the door, running with no direction. Bailey knew he was running out of time so he ended the soap opera.

"Bye Tiffany, and oh yeah, your pussy was great; we should get together sometime and make a flick."

Tiffany's eyes start pouring tears faster than someone pouring milk in their favorite cereal in the morning. She pulled on Bailey's pants, as she pleaded on her knees, "Please don't leave me, please don't let me be a broken hearted girl, please I can't play that role."

"Tiffany, get up and have some dignity. Where did you get that from?" Rhonda said to Tiffany in her high pitched voice.

Bailey looked down at Tiffany, shaking his head. The fact that she was begging him boosted his ego up. "Girl your ass should be in Hollywood somewhere. You don't want me; you want the hype that comes with me. Now get your stupid ass off me so I can go catch my girl."

Bailey ran out the door, hoping that Zakiya wasn't too far for him to catch up and to his surprise there she was running down the long dirt road that headed to her house. "Yo Zakiya, wait up shawty."

Zakiya stopped running and turned towards Bailey to say, "Fuck you Bailey."

"Come on baby don't be like that, stay right there so we can talk." Zakiya stood there waiting for Bailey to catch up. With a vulnerable face, her lips were shaking, and her eyes were semi-wet, Zakiya looked as if she could fall apart at any moment. "Baby I am sorry. I know that's not enough for what I've done to you but I'm still going to let you know that I'm sorry. I promise you it was nothing more than a fucking nut. She came on to me so I allowed her to make an ass out of herself."

Zakiya looked at Bailey as he pleaded, shaking her head at his pathetic act, gaining the strength from him begging to give him the words he was asking for. "You brought this on yourself Bailey so like the saying goes, 'You made your bed now lay in it.' Do you think that I want you back after this? You embarrassed me and my family. People in church are going to be talking about this, our friends from school and everything. I'm supposed to take you back with open arms? You can have that BITCH because like the song says I'm chunking my deuces at your stupid ass. That bitch doesn't want you. She wants what comes with you. In case you didn't know, a bitch always wants what a bitch can't have or what another bitch got. When she sees that I'm not with your ass, Bailey, and she gets around all them fine ass older football players at ASU, she is going to forget about your stupid ass.

"Nigga I loved you for real, now look at you standing here looking like a bitch left with his dick in his hand. I'm young, smart, beautiful, and can count on my hands how many niggas I have been with. News flash, ONE! Do you know how many niggas would die to have me as their girl?" Zakiya answered her own question, "I do, a motherfucking million and counting, nigga."

"Zakiya don't get your ass whooped now, talking all this shit."

"Nigga you not going to put your hands on me, you not that stupid."

Bailey walked swiftly towards Zakiya as if he was about to take all the stress Zakiya had just given him out on her face. He clenched his fists in anger. You could see the veins in his forehead. "Girl, you better find you somebody to play with on some real shit."

Zakiya jumped, putting her hands in front of her face as Bailey walked towards her, raising his voice aggressively. When she saw he wasn't going to hit her, she started cursing him out again, letting go of all the words she could think of, hoping it would heal her broken heart faster. "I did find somebody. I'm playing with him right now. I treat little boys like little boys. You want to act like a dumb ass child, I am going to talk to you like a boy, Bailey. Now get the fuck out of my face nigga before I have you seen about. Since the bitch's pussy was so good, go marry her then, I am good. I did all the crying I'm going to do over your sorry ass." Zakiya voice weakens but she did her best to fight back the tears.

"Man, you taking this shit way out of proportion." Bailey stepped back to look Zakiya in her face, he couldn't believe how far she was taking the conflict.

"I'm taking it way out of proportion? Zakiya clapped her hands together making them sound off. Really Bailey, when you're the fucking one who fucked a girl who I have never gotten along with at a fucking party with everybody who knows me. You give motherfucukers a reason to laugh at me. I hate you for this shit Bailey. Both of Zakiya hands pushed into Bailey's chest. Bailey puffed up and blew out hot air, rubbing his hand down his face trying to wipe the anger away. "You just don't know the feeling I got when I heard this bullshit. It was like my heart had been ripped out by my best friend's man. Do you know how that feels? Of course not because I have never done you like that Bailey.

Never in a million years would I even think about doing you that way. I've always saved myself for you, ALWAYS! Never again, not no more, the good girl has left the building. From now on I am only fucking with niggas that are worthy, so the next time I am hurt at least he paid for the shit in advance. You taught me a valuable lesson so I thank you. Never fuck with a broke ass nigga who only have love to offer you." Zakiya starts clapping her hands. "And the buster award goes to that broke lying nigga standing, all my broke niggas please stand up."

Bailey made the ugliest face as he told Zakiya, "Girl shut up with all that shit, waking up the got damn neighborhood."

"Why, they going to find out anyway Bailey. I might as well be the one to tell them. My nigga cheated on me with a groupie whore." Zakiya rolled her eyes as she finished up her conversation in the calmest tone of the night, saying, "You pathetic you know that? You don't ever have to worry about me again Bailey. I'm gone, there is no more you and me. I just can't see myself being with you after you've been with her. Then you stayed with the bitch for a whole weekend, man. Talking about it was just the sex. So what you had to lay up with the bitch the whole weekend? You just said fuck me Bailey."

"Man it's not even like that Zakiya I'm telling you. The only one who's going to be embarrassed is her for fucking me around everybody."

"Well you will never have me so I guess she will never be embarrassed."

Bailey took a step back from Zakiya, asking her, "So that's how you want it to be?"

Zakiya stared Bailey directly in the eye, "Yelp, that's how it is Bailey." Zakiya's heart was pounding. She was breaking it off with the only boy she ever loved and been with in her life. She turned away, walking off so that Bailey wouldn't catch that she was just as hurt as he was.

"Bye Zakiya, and remember no matter what, I still love you and I always will."

BIG DREAMS

The day was young, so Zakiya decided to walk back to town so that she could get her Visa card that held access to her lottery winnings. Walking back from the bank, she decided to stop by Eva's house to tell her the plans she had for them. When Zakiya reached Eva's burnt orange and brown house, her strength was weak from crying all the way there thinking about Bailey. Tap, tap, tap," you could barely hear the knocks.

"Who is it?"

"It's me Eva."

Eva opened the door when she heard Zakiya's voice.

"Hey honey, I didn't know you were coming over."

Zakiya tried to fix the sadness in her voice so that Eva wouldn't see that she had been crying. "Yeah honey, I need to talk to you about some things."

"Oh really, about what?"

Zakiya walked in Eva's house, heading up the stairs, signaling Eva to follow her. Zakiya reached Eva's room and closed the door. Sitting herself on the end of Eva's queen size bed, she got straight to the point. "If you had a chance to move out of this town, would you move and where to?"

"Why?"

"Just answer the question Ms. Thing."

"I don't think I will move to be honest, Zakiya. Although this town has its boring moments and can gossip up a storm, I love it. To me, this is home. However, I do plan on visiting other places, not to stay though, only to vacay. I would miss this town too much to move. It's like it's got a spell on the people who are born here. Why? Where would you go if you had the money to move?" Eva asked, looking Zakiya directly in the eyes.

"I think I will go to New York. I always desired to become a writer, you know."

"Yeah you always wanted to write novels."

"So I would move there and start me a business first, so that I could support my writing career."

"Yeah, but what kind of business?"

"One that would boom. I like shoes so maybe I will open a shoe store or something. Matter of fact, let me use your computer, honey."

Eva pointed at the computer and said "It's right there, why you asking me?"

Zakiya walked over to the computer desk.

"What you up to?"

Zakiya turned to Eva and said, "You can't tell anybody but I'm about to leave Jackson."

Eva raised her eyebrow and asked, "And go where?"

Zakiya responded, "To New York. I talked to Bob and he told me about his cousin who has real estate up there. He said that he will give me a good deal on one of the properties that was foreclosed and the good thing about it is the property that he is talking about giving me is in Manhattan."

Eva nodded her head while saying, "That's what's up. There's only one problem with that, how the hell you going to get the money to get the property and to keep it?"

Zakiya looked at Eva and said, "Believe child, have faith. I will. I just have to put on my hustling ball cap."

Eva burst out laughing at Zakiya's comment. "What the hell made you wake up and think of all this?"

"I told you I want to get out of this town. Plus I can easily open up a book store mixed with a coffee shop that sells bagels and little finger foods. I will call it The Lounge."

Eva looked at Zakiya with her arms folded and said, "Well haven't you been dreaming. I thought you said a shoe store."

"Yeah, but I just thought about it and a bookstore would be better since I want to become an author. And yes Eva I got big dreams and I'm going to turn them into reality you will see. I can see me now, closet full of shoes like Carrie living the Sex in the City life. So I am going to ask you again, are you down?" Zakiya tilted her head to the side with her right eyebrow raised.

"You never asked me that, chick, but if you talking about leaving, yeah you on your own with that one." Eva said looking at Zakiya questioning face.

"Well I found some vendors with great prices."

"Vendors for what Zakiya?"

"For my book store. I want to sell every book and magazine there is. I'm even going to hold book signings at The Lounge. I'm telling you, when I do publish my book, I'm going to be a foot ahead of the game."

"Just where do you expect to get the money from to start all of this Zakiya?" Eva said with a smirk on her face.

"Eva, you must tell no one, not even my family." Zakiya voice lowered and her face went from calm to serious.

"Now you are scaring me."

"I hit the lottery Eva."

She couldn't make out Zakiya's face. She stood there with her mouth wide open. "Girl, are you for real?"

"Yes I'm dead ass serious."

"Oh my God!" Eva walked towards Zakiya, hugging her tight.

"Don't tell anybody, I trust you."

Eva stepped back from Zakiya and said, "Ok secret agent, I won't. Dang! So you really are planning on leaving, aren't you?"

"Yelp!"

"What about your boosky?"

"Fuck that mother fucker!" Zakiya sounded like a mad chipmunk.

Eva tooted her lips and said, "I guess you heard?"

"So you knew and you didn't tell me Eva!"

Eva's heart dropped and realized that her friend might have taken that move as a betrayal play. "Yes I knew, but I wasn't going to be the one to tell you some shit like that. I just couldn't bring the words out of my mouth. I even picked up the phone and was about to call you, but my mother said that you might have taken it as me hating on you because you got a man and I don't."

Zakiya shook her head. "Eva, I would have never thought about it that way. I so wish it could have been you who told me instead of Robert. Do you know how embarrassing that was?"

Eva shook her head. "I can only imagine. I can't say I know."

"I forgive you though. I guess I can see it from your point of view."

"So how did you find out?" Eva hurried up and said, "Oh that's right, you said Robert. So did you confront him?"

"Girl did I. I went to that bitch's sister's house acting an ass, cursing all their asses out."

"Oh my God, no you didn't Zakiya."

"Oh yes the hell I did. Once I finished cursing him out, he cursed her out."

Eva started laughing so hard she had to grab her stomach. "Damn bitch, I guess you get that part from your daddy."

Zakiya responded, "I guess I do, because my momma would have said that's for hood rats with no class."

"So yawl two are over or you going to give him another chance?"

"Nawl I'm through and on to the next one, like the song say."

"So when you plan on leaving?"

"Soon Eva, very soon. Bob's cousin said if I wanted the property, I'd better hurry up because there are other people dying to get it. I'm going to pack tonight and then I'm out of here."

Eva's voice rose higher than before. "Damn that fast, Zakiya!"

"Yeah, I want to be gone and go while it's hot so I can see what I am dealing with. I am going to buy my business license from this guy Bob knows just in case I want to open up something else."

Eva twisted her head in a circular motion. "Go on then Ms. Thing. I wish you much success baby and I am so happy for you, but I can't help but be selfish."

Eva said with a puppy dog face, "Selfish how, Eva?"

"Because I want to ask you to stay, I don't want you to go and leave me."

"I told your ass to come with me, but nawl you want to stay in this small ass no direction town." Zakiya was sarcastic and sad all at once. "So when I get stable, I'll be calling you." Both hands on her hips, down, then on her hips again, Zakiya paced the floor.

"At least you can come visit me."

"Of course, chick, I can do that." Zakiya leaned towards Eva who was only a foot away and hugged her tight. "I am going to make sure I call you as soon as I get to the big city."

Eva hugged Zakiya just as tightly. "You better chick or I'm going to be mad with your ass. Don't get up there and forget about me either."

"Oh I can never do that, this are my roots. I just want to get established first, then I wouldn't mind coming back to the town for holidays and things."

"I feel you, I guess. I just know I can't be mad at you for wanting more."

Zakiya finally turned Eva loose. "I knew you would understand. I just don't know if I am going to be able to say the same about my family, especially my momma."

"Girl she is going to have a fit. Zakiya, what are you going to tell her?"

"The same thing I told you, I got to get out and explore. I am grown so there is nothing she can do about it. All she could do is accept it and pray for me and you know she is a Christian, so she got to forgive me."

"Well I wish you nothing but blessings honey."

"Thanks friend, now let me get out of here. The quicker I talk to my momma the better." The girls hugged one last time before Zakiya rushed down the stairs leaving the door open behind her.

Eva stood in the door watching her best friend walk away.

Zakiya turns around facing Eva after realizing she forgot to tell her best friend to lie for her. "Eva, if any of my sisters or my mother asks you, tell them I'm going to stay with our friend from school in New York."

"Ok you little sneaky heifer." Eva smiled at Zakiya learning how to lie shaking her head side-to-side.

"Thank you, love." Five minutes later, Zakiya was home. The moment Zakiya walked in her mother's front door, her heart dropped to her knees.

"Where you been honey?" Harmony asked Zakiya.

"Taking care of some business, where is momma?"

Harmony shoved her shoulder and said, "I don't know, why?"

"Well come to the sitting room, I got news to tell everyone,"

"About what?" Harmony asked.

"If you go to the sitting room you will see," Zakiya didn't plan on repeating herself. Harmony skipped to the seating area like a little kid.

"Calling everybody to the living room, calling everybody to the living room, family meeting." Zakiya joked as she loudly made the announcement, walking down the hallway,

"Yayy! Family meeting!" Maddison screamed as she ran to the living room.

Mary walked out her room looking at Zakiya as she screamed loudly about a family meeting. "Child why are you making all that noise?"

"Momma, I got some important news I need to tell everyone, so can you please go to the living room?"

"Now you are scaring me. What has happened Zakiya?"

"Nothing has happened Momma, calm down. It's nothing to be scared about."

Mary cut her eyes at Zakiya, wondering what it was that had Zakiya in such a good mood. Walking to the living room together, they joined the others who were anxiously waiting to hear the news that had Zakiya up and out the house bright and early. Zakiya stood in front of the living room while her sisters and mother sat on the couch patiently waiting.

"Well I just talked to my great friend from school that just recently got a job with Simon & Schuster publishing company. She put in a good word for me and got me a three month internship there."

Mary quickly snapped with her arms folded, "And where does this friend live?"

"New York."

Cambria rolled her eyes and said, "Girl you don't know nothing about no damn New York. Don't you know it is expensive to just stay in the poorest area of that city?"

"Watch your mouth Cambria," Mary said. "But your sister is right, Zakiya. You can't afford to live in New York. It's too expensive."

"I know that's why I will be sharing an apartment with my friend who has her own place. It's a paid internship so that way I can pay her for staying there. I have made up my mind I'm going and no one can stop me. I just thought I would be mature and responsible by letting yawl know. I'm leaving tonight. Everything is already set up so I will call yawl when I reach the Big Apple."

Layla asked, "Why so fast Zakiya?"

"Because my plane leaves tonight, Layla."

"You don't tell your mother what you going to do. You ask her first. Are you out your damn mind or something?" Cambria snapped at Zakiya. She was the oldest and the closest to her mother. She even had the Christian ways like her mother.

Harmony took up for Zakiya because it seemed as if she was about to explode. "That girl is grown, Cambria, she can do whatever it is she wants to do. Not everyone wants to stay in this boring ass town all their life. How are you going to put her down for wanting to do more and see more out of life? If you want to stay here all your life and have kids with the white picket fence then fine, but this girl has always wanted to be a writer. How dare you put her dream down like that. You and momma should be more supportive. I just can't figure out what kind of Christians are yawl."

Mary got up and walked off with tears in her eyes. "Harmony, you are the devil." How could you talk about your mother that way?" Layla said rolling her eyes.

"I'm not talking to her in no way Cambria. I wish yawl would see that everyone has different dreams and just because it's not the dream you dream every night doesn't mean it's the wrong one."

Melody stood up off the beige love seat she was sitting on and said, "All this screaming is getting on my nerves and plus yawl no momma can't take all this excitement."

Melody turned to Zakiya and said, "I wish you luck honey, call us when you get there and let us know how it is." Once Melody said what she had to say she walked off heading toward her Momma's master bedroom.

"Well I wish you luck too honey and don't forget about us when you get up there and make it big," Layla said. After Layla said her peace she got off the beige two; seater sofa and walked down the hall to her and Maddison's bedroom.

Zakiya walked toward Harmony and whispered "thank you" in her ear. Harmony nodded her head and said, "Honey, have fun, leave the regrets at the door.

Make sure you call me and tell me how the Big Apple is really like. Of course you would have to get my new number from Mother then, because I will not be here for long either. In fact I'm leaving by the end of the summer."

"I'm happy for you Harmony and I wish you and Jesse much happiness."

"Thank you, little sister."

"Now let's go apologize to Momma," Zakiya said. They both walked off heading to their mother's room tapping on the door softly trying to see if it was safe to enter. "Come in girls."

Zakiya and Harmony sat in the middle of the bed that was covered with a homemade, stitched quilt that her and her mother Annabella sewed together.

"Momma, I'm sorry if I hurt your feelings because I love you, but I will not apologize for how I feel." Harmony said with a soft voice.

"I know Harmony. That's what I always admired about you. You always had that will power, that cockiness. I guess you got that from your father."

Zakiya interrupted and said, "I'm sorry too, Momma."

"Yawl don't have to apologize. I understand, it's just that I fear for yawl. I know what's out there in this scary world. Do y'all think I always wanted to stay here in Jackson all my life? I explored the world and when I did it was a disaster. All I could do was wish I never left home."

"But Momma you got to let us make our mistakes because that's the only way we will learn." Harmony said as Zakiya nodded her head.

"I know that now Harmony, but at the end of the day I'm still your mother and I will forever protect yawl. Until you have kids, you will never understand."

"We understand, Momma," Harmony said. Mary knew there was no horror story scary enough for Zakiya to stay. She wanted out of Jackson so bad, Mary didn't bother telling Zakiya about her scary adventure.

Zakiya saw that the mood in the room was at ease and she wanted to get out of there before it switched. So she kissed her mother on the cheek and said, "I will call you as soon as I land." Zakiya jumped off the bed skipping to her room feeling nothing but joy in her heart. She was so glad the hard part was out of the way. Zakiya had to be at the airport by 10:00 p.m. that night, so she packed her bags so she would be ready when Mr. Bob came to get her.

Zakiya couldn't believe she was leaving Jackson so soon. She was packing like she was in a world packing contest. Zakiya wasn't even going to miss home. The thought of coming back scared her. She was ready to take on New York. To her it was going to be an adventure. For years Zakiya dreamed about living in New York. She watched every episode of Sex in the City more than ten times and Carrie, a smart, successful writer with a mean shoe game, was her inspiration. Layla watched as Zakiya packed like New York was going to leave her.

"Well aren't you packing fast? You not going to be scared living up there all by yourself?" Layla asked.

"I am not going to be by myself."

"I mean you know, not having some family to talk to, you don't even know nothing about New York. Or do you? Because I know I wouldn't just up and go to a city as big as New York without carefully thinking it through. Have you been thinking about this Zakiya?" Layla was curious and slightly sad that her partner in crime was moving.

"I'm going to call you chicks every time I get a chance. We are going to be on the phone all the time." Zakiya comforted Layla with a handful of lies and ignored her questions so she wouldn't be accused of lying. She had no intentions on keeping up with the updates of Jackson once she moved. The plan was to settle in and enjoy being single and independent before checking in with home constantly. Zakiya was ready to be in a house where she didn't have to share anything.

THE CONFRONTATION

Jarlath looked up at the ceiling while lying in his king sized bed as his maid opened the curtains to the four feet windows that were to the left of him. "Good morning Jarlath, how did you sleep?" Lisa kept a professional swag about herself, she tried not to let the affair she had with her boss affect her work

"I'm fine, how is my messy wife doing?"

Alayne had been back from the hospital for about a week now but she was on bed rest so Jarlath made her sleep in the guest room down the hall.

"She is doing much better now, Jarlath. Would you like for me to tell her something for you?"

Jarlath sat up on the bed facing Lisa. "Nawl I'm heading her way in a minute."

"Ok. Well I will be downstairs if you need me." Lisa responded.

Jarlath did his morning stretch looking out the tall windows with a blank face before walking into his multi-storied million dollar walk-in closet. He decided that he wasn't going to put on a suit for today. Instead he pulled out his Seven Jeans, a white V-neck T-shirt and a Gucci scarf. He could pull off a suit or jeans with his swag. There was nothing that didn't look sexy on him.

After Jarlath finished dressing, he went to the guest room where his wife was laying. The moment Jarlath walked into the room, her heart dropped. Jarlath had been giving Alayne the cold shoulder since she arrived from the hospital. Not once did he come into the room to check on her. Alayne knew he was furious with her for trying to kill herself. There was one thing Jarlath hated the most and that was the media being in his business. He knew that the media could do some damage to his career if his lifestyle was ever truly leaked, and Alayne's suicide attempt was a key for the media to open the gate that led to his house. Alayne's eyes were opened wide when Jarlath approached her.

"Are you well, wife?" Alayne didn't answer, knowing Jarlath really didn't want an answer. "Do you know the embarrassment you caused me doing what you did?"

Alayne was about to say sorry, but she was cut off by Jarlath. "No need to answer. What's done is done, but I just want you to know this. Your fun ended when Kilo died."

Alayne raised her eyebrows slightly, fixating her wet eyes on Jarlath. She was shocked to hear that Jarlath knew about Kilo. Fear was an understatement to describe how Alayne felt. She tucked her shaking hands between her thighs under the covers. She knew from that point on, her life was going to be a living hell.

"From now on, I will do what I want, when I want, and I dare you to question me. I tried to treat you like a queen, but you treated yourself like a whore and no need to run for safety. There will be no divorce until I get ready."

Taking a deep breath, Alayne prepped herself for the torture she knew was ahead. "If I hear about you being with another man, your career and your life as you know it will be ripped from you. You will be back at square one, broker than a New York bomb." Jarlath wanted to waste no time with the torturing process.

"Lisa," Jarlath called. Lisa dropped the duster at the sound of Jarlath voice and swiftly walked to the room across the hall. "Yes Jarlath?"

Jarlath leaned toward Lisa and stuck his tongue down her mouth, sucking on her lips. Alayne's heart was covered in pain as she watched the man she still loved tongue kiss her maid.

After two minutes of passionate kissing, Jarlath tongue washed his lips before he said, "And yes, I have been fucking her for quite a while," turning towards Alayne, hoping he cut her the same way she cut him when he found out about her affair with Kilo.

Khalon: Missing Pieces

"Chris Paul tallied 24 points and 12 assists to lead the Clippers to their first division title in franchise history with a 109-85 win over the Lakers." ESPN watched Khalon while he napped, stretched out across the black, leather Le Corbusier sofa with scattered clippings of newspaper articles about Kilo's murder in his lap. Khalon tried hard to keep his eyes open, but the long nights working the case was finally catching up to him. He was only sleep for a good twenty minute before his cell phone rang waking him up.

"Detective Khalon," Khalon answered with static in his voice.

"I didn't catch you at a bad time did I?" the young lady asked. Khalon sat up on the sofa and looked at the number on the phone.

"Who is this?"

"Hey, this is Kelly. I got your number from you Captain. Are you busy?" I know he did not give this girl my number. Damn! Khalon thought shaking his head looking at the number on his cell screen.

"No, I'm not busy. I just dosed off for a minute. The long nights are catching up with me. This is Kelly right?"

Khalon said wiping his face.

"Yes, this is Kelly. I'm sorry to wake you. I know how it can be sometimes."

"Oh you fine. I'm up now."

"Have you eaten anything?"

"SHIT! Hold up for a second sweety." Khalon jumped up off the sofa and ran to the kitchen with the phone in his hand. He completely forgot about the store bought Salisbury steaks he put in the oven.

"I forgot about my damn food." Khalon said holding the phone to his ear with one hand and trying to fan the smoke from the oven with other hand.

"Now how you do that?" Kelly asked with a high pitch voice.

"I fell asleep and forgot about them and the messed up part about it is I already had them in the oven for about fifth-teen minutes before I dosed off. I was trying to get them a little more done."

Joking around Kelly responded, "Well, they are done now."

"Yes they are all the way done. Now, I got to air my house out."

"Well, this is my number. You can just lock me in and give me a call when you are free, okay?"

"Cool, I'll do just that."

"Okay, bye Khalon," "One." Khalon had no intentions on calling Kelly back.

αααα

Knock, knock, knock. Lisa taps on Alayne's bedroom door were soft and short. Before she could get to the fourth knock, Alayne screamed out, "What? C!" "You have a call, would you like for me to tell them to call you back?" Lisa didn't want to step a foot in Alayne's room. She was too embarrassed. Getting kissed by Jarlath in front her, in her home, was very disrespectful. A part of Lisa wanted to kill Jarlath for making things awkward between her and Alayne, but the other part of her was flattered. Alayne snapped at Lisa, slamming her remote down afterwards. "You can give me the damn phone, then dismiss yourself immediately. That's what you can do for me. Give me the damn phone, then you can dismiss yourself before I beat the shit out of you, you whore!" Lisa set the phone on the bed and walked out of Alayne' room swiftly.

"Hello!" Alayne screamed in the phone.

"Hey Alayne, this is Sandy."

"Who?" "Sandy, Kilo's girlfriend." Alayne's heart dropped to her feet. Kilo told her before he was murdered that he broke off his relationship with Sandy. Alayne paused for a minute then said, "Hey, how are you?" "I'm not doing so good. I miss my love but I'll pull through with God's help." Alayne rolled her eyes. She didn't care to hear how Sandy really felt, she was just trying to be polite. Ready to get to the point of the phone call, Alayne asked, "Was it something you needed?"

Quickly Sandy responded, "Oh no, I mean well yeah, kind of." Alayne shook her head thinking, I knew it was something.

"See, here is the thing. Kilo and I were going through some things, you know?"

Sandy waited for a response but Alayne left her dry. So she continued.

"I think he was cheating on me but I didn't have proof. The nigga could lie like his life depended on it. Anyway's, I had an investigator's following him and they told me the last time they seen Kilo, he was in Central Park, being pulled over by the police. They said he didn't have a girl in the car, but to make a long story short, can you get one of your high price lawyers to find the cop that pulled my man over? Because he was the last one to see him alive and I'm going to get some Justice for my man." You could hear the chewing gum popping while Sandy talked. Alayne stayed quite, secretly trying to piece clues together but she couldn't think straight with the gum popping and Sandy talking her ear off. "I'm defiantly going to let Jarlath know about this, in fact let me call you back Sandy as soon as I talk to my husband." Alayne had no intentions on calling Jarlath but she would say anything to get off the phone with Sandy.

As soon as she hit the end button on the cordless phone, she grabbed her white Chanel purse off the night stand and got detective Khalon's card out. Alayne couldn't risk him having her house number so she called him private and after three rings he answered.

"Hello, hello."

"Hey, this is Alayne I got…"

"This who?" Khalon asked cutting Alayne off. Quickly Alayne responded, "It's me, Alayne."

"I told you to stop calling me private. I wasn't just talking for my health when I said that."

"I'm not calling about that. I think I might have you a witness for that case you're working on." Khalon pressed the blackberry to his ear. "What you mean a witness?" The tone of Alayne's voice changed. sShe started whispering on the phone.

"I'm going to write it all down in an email and send it to you. I don't want to talk about on the phone. I'm at home, my husband might hear." Khalon nodded his head, "oh right do that, bye." Alayne hung up the phone. Then Lisa hung up the kitchen phone she was listening in on.

THE BIG CITY

Zakiya touched down in JFK International Airport inhaling the smoggy air the big city offered. She was only fifteen miles away from Manhattan where her soon to be Lounge was going to open. Dressed in a white skirt, Zakiya's mini and chiffon blouse cover the essentials and accentuated the positive as she twisted her round ass outside the airport where the cabs waited. Her hands were full, rolling two of her knock off Gucci suitcase with a tote bag on her shoulders.

Zakiya wanted to start her new life off fresh, so she brought as little luggage as possible. Stepping to the curb where the cab waited, she hit the trunk signaling that the cab driver should pop the trunk.

"2012 Manhattan St. please." Zakiya demanded before jumping in.

"Yes ma'am." The cab driver could see the excitement on Zakiya face when he glanced at her through his mirror. "First time in New York ma'am?" the cab driver asked, looking through his rearview mirror.

"Yes, I'm here to get some of the New York action."

The cab driver laughed. "What do you do for a living, if you don't mind me asking?"

"No, I don't." Zakiya inhaled, then exhaled before answering, "I am an author."

"Oh okay. Pretty young, I like that. You sound very ambitious" The cab driver shook his head yes, with his eyes glued to the road.

"Oh, I am. There is success out there with my name on it." Zakiya said looking out the window.

"I hear you. There's nothing wrong with that. So are you from New York?" Zakiya asked the cab driver who looked old enough to be an older uncle.

"Yelp, born and raised."

"Any advice for me?"

"Only stay to yourself and trust no one."

Zakiya nodded her head. "That sounds good to me."

"Well we are here missy. Would you like me to wait for you?"

"Um," Zakiya said, hesitating, not knowing if she should let the cab driver leave before she checked out the store.

"I think I will be fine. Sorry, I didn't get your name. What is it?"

"I'm Ronny. I drive this area pretty often so I'm sure this won't be the last time we run into each other."

"Okay, great. Well I am Zakiya."

"That's a beautiful name. Nice to meet you, Zakiya."

"Same here, Ronny." Zakiya handed the driver a twenty, leaving him a five dollar tip. She stood on the sidewalk with her luggage, taking a minute to look at the moving traffic. Everyone was moving in a direction or going somewhere. It was beautiful. No one was speaking to each other or even mad that their presence wasn't acknowledged, unlike Zakiya's home in the south. In the south, every car that drove by blew their horn, throwing up their hands. Everyone spoke even if they didn't know the person. The southern hospitality was somewhat annoying and old to Zakiya and she was enjoying the rudeness and cockiness New York offered. Zakiya looked towards the sky to view the top of the tall buildings as the light, cool wind blew her skirt. The summer in New York felt like a warm breeze, versus the hot, humid south, where you could wear a swim suit for an outfit and still be hot.

Enjoying the breeze, Zakiya blindly searched her purse for the keys to her newly owned building. She received the keys from Bob when he came to take her to the airport.

Zakiya had given the money to Bob to give to his cousin and just like that, she owned her building. Now all she needed to do was bring the life she envisioned for it to reality. Zakiya walked up the five sets of stairs that led to the front door of the building, then entered into the empty building that echoed. Looking around, she felt like a million bucks. The building was very spacious and held an apartment on top of the store that was also Zakiya's. She smiled from ear to ear, thanking God for her blessing. Zakiya knew that staying in New York was expensive, so she was getting the best deal, a shop and a place to stay, all in one. Ms. Independent walked to the back of the room and opened a door that looked like a closet. There she saw the stairs that led to the apartment part of the building. Looking around, Zakiya was very pleased. It was just enough room for a single aspiring author.

The large, one bedroom studio apartment was fully equipped; dishwasher, hardwood floors with lots of light, small open to the city views, new bathroom and kitchen. There was central A/C and great closet space. Zakiya felt like the luckiest girl in the world. To get a studio that didn't need too much maintenance was great and it was all hers. All she had to do was pay the taxes which she chose to pay yearly.

Once Zakiya took a long tour of her studio, she went back down to where the Lounge was. She walked into the small Kitchen. Zakiya wished it could have been bigger, but who was she to complain. Besides, the only thing she was planning on making in there were bagels, hot donuts, and all sorts of hot beverages for cold New York winters.

Zakiya wasn't going to stay in the shop tonight because of the lack of furniture, so she pulled out her new Mac laptop that she purchased before coming to New York, so she could book a room in one of New York's finest hotels. Zakiya wanted to treat herself and celebrate her independence. After booking her room at the New York Palace Hotel, she walked out the building, locking it up, remembering that she was now in New York. Zakiya held her hand out less than a second for a cab. "455 Madison Avenue please," Zakiya said, properly and professionally, enjoying the feeling of being grown and on her own. The cab driver wasn't like the first one. He drove Zakiya directly to her destination, and said absolutely nothing.

"That will be ten seventy-five ma'am." Zakiya gave the cab driver eleven dollars and off to the Palace she went. The New York Palace Hotel is known for luxurious accommodations, spectacular views, and personalized service. So Zakiya was excited about the stay, plus the Palace was located in the heart of NYC near Rockefeller Center and world class shopping.

"Welcome to the Palace Hotel, ma'am. Do you have a reservation?"

"Yes, Zakiya Parker."

"Sure, I have you right here." The receptionist handed Zakiya her key and Zakiya just wanted to faint. She was still in amazement about being in the most talked about city on her own.   Zakiya knew New York was the place for her to be a successful writer and live life on the edge all in one.

She walked into her suite and it was amazing. The room came with plush bedding with 100% cotton sheets and marble bathrooms with great bathrobes, spacious seating, work areas and for a surcharge, she had secure high-speed internet. Zakiya had her room for a week which meant she had to get busy with making plans for building a studio home. This didn't worry her at all. Zakiya had it all figured out.

Zakiya Sat at the desk Googling the furniture store she had seen on TV back home, Altin Furniture, delivered all over the USA as long as you paid. Since the furniture wasn't that pricey but was great quality, Zakiya decided to give them a try. She didn't mind paying the delivery fee after seeing the prices in New York furniture stores. Altin's delivery fee plus furniture, was nowhere close to just furniture minus the delivery in New York. After Zakiya ordered furniture for both the studio and The Lounge, she unpacked, ready to grub.

She was alone, so Zakiya didn't want to go outside the hotel to eat so she decided to dine at The Palace's very own Gilt - Two Michelin Star restaurant located just inside the courtyard gates of the Villard Mansion. There was a large wine selection, including wines by the glass. The Gilt served cuisine in an inventive, modern American opulent setting of gilded walls and cathedral ceilings. Sitting alone with her thoughts at ease, Zakiya waited for the waitress she sent off only minutes ago because she wasn't ready.

"Are you ready to order ma'am or do you want me to give you a little more time?"

"No, I'm ready. I'll have the sirloin steak with melted cheddar cheese, sour crème and bacon."

"Okay, would you like broccoli and cheese, baked potato, or both?"

"Both."

"Sure, what would you like to drink with that?"

"Sweet tea, please, thank you," Zakiya said to the pretty, slim African American waitress.

Ten minutes later, the waitress was back at Zakiya's table with her food. Zakiya sat and ate her delicious dinner still not believing how lucky she was. Watching the couples eat didn't even make Zakiya wish she had a man. It only gave her the motivation she needed to succeed in her goals. Zakiya had a plan and it was the bomb.

She was going to get on her feet, get her Lounge bumping, take some of her profit and self-publish her first book. Once she had at least four to five novels out, she would then hunt for a man. Zakiya knew there was nothing like a woman with her own identity and she didn't see herself without one. She was already smart, young, and beautiful so her next step was to work on her career. Zakiya knew that in order to play and live comfortably you have to be dedicated and you have to work smart.

After eating the delicious meal, Zakiya walked back to her room, feeling great. There was nothing that could tear her spirit and the smile on her face said it all. Zakiya spoke to every person she passed in the hallway on the way to her room, which wasn't too common in the busy city but Zakiya didn't care. She was in good a mood. Her plan for the night was to rent some movies off Comcast and fall asleep watching them, wrapped in nothing but her white robe. She felt more comfortable sleeping naked. She just wasn't allowed to back home because of the number of people and lack of privacy.

NEW FRIENDS

On the way back to her room, Zakiya saw a pretty, young Latina girl in the hall crying with her head on the cleaning cart. She wondered if she should ask if she was alright but then realized she could no longer be the sweet southern girl who cared for others. The last thing she wanted was to try and help a stranger and then get herself into some danger.

Zakiya stuck her key in her door and said to the crying broken heart girl, "Will you bring me some towels and scented candles in when you finish. Thanks." Zakiya said to the girl in a sarcastic tone while tooting her rear up, twirling her purse, standing back on her nude suede Stilettos. The young Latina girl who looked to be at least twenty-five, stared at Zakiya like she wanted to dish out every curse word she could think of.

The 5'4 Latina stood up, wiping her tears away, looked Zakiya up and down as if she was saying in her mind you rich stuck up bitch. "Sure I will. Is there any particular candles you looking for?"

"No anything that smells good will be great." The Latina girl reached below her cleaning cart pulled out the cinnamon scented air wick candles and grabbed the white, fluffy towels off the top of the cart rack, and walked into Zakiya's room catering to her request. Zakiya watched the maid whose name tag read Saran pack her towels in the bathroom.

"Do you feel better now?" Zakiya asked in a very harsh tone.

"I'm fine and sorry about that. I didn't mean for you to see that. ma'am."

"Don't ma'am me. Do I look like I'm old enough to be a ma'am to you?" Zakiya snapped at the maid quickly. "How old are you anyway?"

"I'm twenty-five. I'm sorry if I offended you."

"Apology accepted. Now what was it that had you so out of it, if you don't mind me asking?"

Holding back on her true thoughts, the maid responded, "Oh, it was nothing." The maid was silent in loss of words of what to call the young, beautiful but arrogant girl.

"Nothing don't have you crying that way and my name is Zakiya."

"Oh that's a beautiful name."

Zakiya ignored saying thank you, leaving the room silent for a second.

"My roommate was just laid off and now I'm suspended from work for being late trying to get her to an interview. The rent is due and neither of us have our part, at least not all of it anyway."

Zakiya thought Saran's situation couldn't be better for her. "Well I am opening a new book store in Manhattan if you or your friends are interested. I am not offering much, however, as time goes by your pay will raise. I am looking for good customer service and people who I do not have to tell what to do. It's a new business and there will be no limitations to your job description. Anything that needs to be done could be your job."

Saran looked at Zakiya with a joyous smile and said, "Thank you so much. I really appreciate this."

Zakiya looked at Saran very snobbily and replied with a strict, cynical tone, "Don't thank me. You have your work cut out for you. So do you think you could do the job?"

"Yes, yes I can."

"And your friend?"

"Yes, she can as well."

Zakiya took a piece of hotel paper off the nightstand and wrote down the address to the store. "Here is the address, now give me your number and when I get ready for you both, which will be soon, I will call you."

Saran took the paper proudly, repeatedly saying "You will not regret this, I promise."

"Words are silent to me. Now actions I hear those so don't worry. Your time to show me how thankful you are will come." Zakiya said to Saran as she opened her room door, signaling that she was finished with the conversation and ready for her leave her room. Saran walked out feeling better than before. The salty girl wasn't so saucy after all Saran thought.

Zakiya lit her candles placing them around the bath tub. In the tub was the richest bubble bath. The Palace provided great bubble bath for their guests and Zakiya was anxious to dive in to enjoy it.

Back home she rarely got to use the Bath and Body Works because of all the girls in the house. One bath a piece, per person was the whole bottle. And she really never got to enjoy a long bath because there was always a line. Zakiya slid off her pink Victoria Secret cheekies and push up bra, laying it on the floor, sitting back in the tub made Zakiya feel like silk. She was on the road to her success and there was nothing that was going to stop her. Everything about the day had her on a high.

The phone rang, startling Zakiya. She was not going to let whoever was on the other end blow her high so she figured she would just call them back.

Knowing it had to be somebody from home wondering if she made it all right, Zakiya decided to ignore the phone call. After all, she didn't forget to call, she just didn't fell like checking in. The day had been so beautiful. She just wanted to enjoy the rest of it in peace. Zakiya was on her own and she felt that she didn't have to check in if she didn't want to. It was her time and she was going to enjoy every piece of it, with no questions asked.

Zakiya didn't care if it angered the others or worried them. For once in her life she wanted to do her own thing, and live her life without someone telling her that it was the wrong way or that she was going to regret the choice. The feeling of not caring felt good. It was almost like a rookie hitting the pipe for the first time. It was something that was very easy to get into and very hard to turn away from. Zakiya understood why New Yorkers took pride in being so cocky and bossy, it felt good.

Zakiya felt that she could never go back home. She just couldn't see herself not getting what she wanted from the great city that never sleeps. Going home would mean failure and it wasn't an option for her.

Zakiya watched as the phone rang. Not wanting to answer it, fearing it would make her feel like she was back home and she didn't want that to happen because it might interfere with her being bossy high. She might get a setback from talking to the controlling Christian mother she had. She hesitated on talking to her family.

"I will call them tomorrow. Hell, I'm relaxing."

Zakiya slept comfortably in the queen size bed. The next day to her, came too quick. The sun shining in Zakiya's room woke her up at 9:00 a.m.. Zakiya could have turned the timer off but she didn't know anything about it. She turned over in her bed for a couple of minutes watching how the tall windows showed her the beautiful Manhattan view. After ten minutes, Hesitant, Zakiya picked up the phone dialing her mother's number and like Zakiya's vision, she picked up on the second ring, worried.

"Hello!" Mary said hysterically.

"Hey, momma."

"Hey Zakiya, how are you?"

"I'm fine, I made it to New York and it's great. I'm sorry I didn't call yawl yesterday but I got so thrown off track. I had to get settled in and that long trip made me sleepy and before I knew, it was the next day."

Mary listened on the phone with her heart pumping sour. She knew her daughter was lying and she knew that this wasn't going to be the last lie she heard from her. The sad part about it was she couldn't do anything. It was out of her hands. "Well glad to hear that you are safe. Your sisters and I were worried sick about you."

"Oh, no need to worry Momma, I'm fine. I just had a lot of things on my plate yesterday. I'm sorry if I scared or worried yawl. But yawl don't have to worry, I will be fine.

Everything so far is going great. I haven't been this happy in my entire life."

Mary wished her baby girl luck. She wanted to end the phone call as quickly as possible because she didn't want Zakiya to hear the hurt in her voice, knowing she would think that she was being over dramatic and negative. "Well baby, I'm about to go lay down. I will call you later or you can just call me if you don't get too caught up."

Zakiya was shocked to hear her mother end the phone call. She thought that she was going to have to make up a lie to get her off the phone. "Okay Momma, and tell everybody I said hey."

"I will."

"Maybe she really is letting go of me." Zakiya said as she opened her suitcase to get out what she wanted to wear for the day.

The hotel phone rang, breaking her train of thought. "Yes?"

"Hello, this is Saran, you met me yesterday."

"I know who you are. What can I do for you?"

"Well my roommate Makeeda has her resume and was wondering if you would like for her to bring it to you today?"

"Sure she can bring it to me, no problem. As a matter of fact, you come with her. I would like to go over some things with yawl."

"Okay would you like for us to meet you at your room?"

"Yes, that will be fine."

"Well, we will be there shortly."

"Okay."

Zakiya hung up the phone and called for room service to bring up a hot breakfast for three. She decided to keep on her white cotton robe since everything that needed to be done was online and didn't require her to go out. The girls wasted no time. "I'm coming," Zakiya said in reply to the knocks on the door. She ran to the door, smiling at the girls, showing both deep dimples, "Oh, wow! Yawl got here fast."

"Yes, we were just around the corner." Saran said.

"This is Makeeda. Makeeda this is Zakiya, our new boss." The tall, dark girl with the long, black Remy weave outstretched her hand and said, "Hey, how are you?" Zakiya gripped her hand firmly and asked if they would come in and have a seat.

The three beautiful girls sat at the table where Zakiya had breakfast laid out for them. "Thank you for this great breakfast." Makeeda said to Zakiya.

"Oh, you both are welcome. Well I'm going to give yawl the basics on what I expect and need to be done. I will be opening the Lounge very soon. The furniture will be arriving soon, along with the books. I will need you two there to set up the bookshelves and furniture.

"The job description is very wide, and not limited. One moment you could be making bagels and coffee, the next you could be a cashier, or stacking books. I will be selling every book and magazine there is so I need to be able to trust that you will not steal from me."

The two girls nodded their heads. "You will not have to worry about us stealing anything from you, you are helping us and we appreciate it." Makeeda said.

"Plus I love to see black on the rise. I think it's a beautiful thing to witness." Makeeda responded with her Brooklyn accent.

"Well, like I told Saran, I don't hear words, but action I see like a motherfucker." Saran and Makeeda looked at each other shocked at the fact that the beautiful young prep-looking girl cursed.

"Where are you from Zakiya?" Makeeda asked Zakiya.

"That doesn't matter." Zakiya said sharply to Makeeda. She didn't want Makeeda to know she was from the sweet southern hospitality state. Plus she didn't want to establish a friendship with an employee.

"Anyway, yawl will start tomorrow. The furniture and the books will be delivered. I want the store ready to open by the end of this week, so that mean we have a lot of work to do ladies. Let's get prepared. A light bulb went off in Makeeda's head.

"I just thought of something. There's a VIP party going down at the 40/40 club and I'm invited. Everyone will be there from authors, to rappers, magazine producers, you name it. It will be a good place to hand out business cards or flyers letting them know that a new book store will be opening." "Makeeda said to Zakiya hoping she could get on her good side.

"Well yeah, sure I will go and I like that. Keep thinking like that. That's the way I want you to think." All kinds of thoughts were going through Zakiya's head. Gosh, I hope I'm able to get in. Dang I hope I don't need I.D. Oh well, I shall see.

"It's a shop two blocks from here that does business cards, postcards and posters for a very good price." Makeeda said.

"If you write down what you want to say on them, me and Saran will be more than happy to go."

Zakiya agreed, walking to the nightstand that held the pencil and pad. She wrote down the information and handed it to them. "What time is this party?"

"It's at 9:00 p.m."

"Okay. Well yawl just bring that back and we can go. I guess it wouldn't hurt. You sure your invitation has plus three on their right?" Zakiya asked turning around toward the girls at the door.

"Yes, I'm sure," Makeeda responded, smiling shaking her 24 inch Remy.

The girls left and Zakiya began searching the web for a good hair stylist. It was time to get a grown look to go with that sexy body. Zakiya quickly walked outside to where there was a fleet of cabs riding the streets and thumbed one down. "Brooklyn Girls Hair Salon please." Zakiya said after jumping in the cab. After listening to the girls with heavy New York accent talk about boys, fashion, and reality shows for an hour, Zakiya was ready to get back to her room so she could get some rest before the girls came. Hours crept past Zakiya as she laid in the very comfortable queen sized bed.

The hotel phone's ringing disturbed Zakiya. She jumped quickly at the first ring, looking at the clock that sat on the stand next to the phone. "Hello."

"Hey Zakiya. It's me, Makeeda."

"Yeah?"

"We are finished with the cards and things, but we're about to stop by our house to get dressed and once we are finished, we will be on our way."

"Okay, that's cool," Zakiya said calmly. Zakiya had taken a bath before taking her nap so she was a step ahead of the girls. She turned on all the lights in the room, pulled out her clothes and looked to see what jaw dropping gear she was going to put on.

Zakiya got a complete makeover at the shop and was anxious to see what luck or man it brought her. Her straight, thick, light candy red hair with side swept bangs went good with her heart-shaped face. Zakiya wanted to turn heads but not scream for attention so she decided to wear her hot pink spandex dress which she believed to be a spicy color that took a lot of confidence to wear. Zakiya slid on the dress to see if it would win the night out and once she looked in the mirror, it was a wrap. The spandex dress did her justice. Showing all the right curves in the right angles, there was no need to take off the dress.

Zakiya slid on her black island platform pumps to seal the deal. With her legs shaved and shiny, make up popping, and body rocking, Zakiya was ready to ball like the rich and sexy do.

Right on time knocking was Makeeda and Lisa. "Come in," Zakiya yelled while looking at the cracked door.

Makeeda and Saran stared at Zakiya who was looking hotter than a paid celebrity. "Damn, don't you look sexy?"

"Thank you," Zakiya replied to Makeeda. "You can just put the posters over there on the table and we can purse some of the business cards." Zakiya looked down at the business cards very pleased.

"Well yawl, let's roll." Zakiya said, walking towards the door. The girls were anxious to party with each other. As soon as they arrived at the party, they immediately saw some of the biggest names in the industry. From Russell Simmons to the Simmons girls, Angela and Vanessa, LL Cool J, Tyra Banks, and more. Zakiya was feeling real hot and was dying to get inside. The moment the girls walked to the front door they were asked for their invitations. Before they could even get them out, the attention of the bouncer went directly to the black MayBach that arrived.

The groupies who were behind the red rope were screaming at the top of their lungs, "I'm glad to see you well! You look amazing!" as the driver opened the door to the industry's favorite couple. Every photographer was snapping uncontrollably. The couple walked towards the girls looking flawless. Jarlath had on an all-black V-neck T-shirt, Sinatra black shades, black cargo jeans, with his nice smell trailing him. Alayne was dressed in a high-fashion see-through jumper, proving why she is several designers' muse.

"Who are they?" Zakiya turned and asked Saran.

"They are only the top paid celebrity couple there is. Makeeda quickly said with her lips tooting at the end of the answer.

"Hey Jarlath and Alayne, how are you two doing today?" he bouncer asked in his ass kissing voice, opening the door for the two to enter.

"Dang, we was here first. We got invitations. Are you going to open the door for us, Mr. Bouncer Man?" Makeeda said in her Brooklyn accent.

Jarlath immediately looked at the three women after Makeeda spoke, very surprised that someone would speak that way towards him while in his presence. "Let the ladies in. In fact yawl can join me in my VIP."

"Now that's what I'm talking about, show a sister some love." Makeeda said nodding her head with her full lips pressed together.

Jarlath laughed at the very outspoken Brooklyn girl. The three of them followed Jarlath in the club like he was their best friend. Alayne had no worries. In fact, she wanted the girls around because of the entertainment Makeeda provided them.

Jarlath took one look at Zakiya and knew she wasn't from New York. Her entire aura told him so. He was always interested in people's stories, where they came from, who they knew, or what they did for a living.

To his benefit, he didn't have to guess for long, "Well, you know my girl is opening up a book store called The Lounge in Manhattan so you should come show her some love if you are ever in the area, which I am sure yawl both are a lot." Makeeda said to Alayne and her husband while giving them Zakiya's business card.

"Is that right?" Jarlath asked.

"Yelp."

"And which one of you girls is opening up a bookstore?"

"I am." Zakiya said in an assured voice. "It's going to be hot, you know somewhere you can get your favorite books or magazines and read while enjoying some good hot coffee, chocolate, latte, or whatever you prefer."

"That's what's up."

"I like that, how old are you?" Jarlath asked.

Ashamed, Zakiya said softly, "Eighteen."

"Damn girl, you young." Makeeda said looking at her future boss with pure shock written all over face.

"Yelp and I'm loving it." Zakiya said with confidence.

"I like you even more now, a young girl with a hustle, that says a lot about you." Jarlath said nodding his head yes.

"I got to stop by and show some love now." Jarlath took both of his hands and put them in his pockets.

"Well I'll be looking forward to it." Zakiya was blushing showing both her dimples.

The girls continued dancing through the night, enjoying all the free drinks Jarlath was offering. After only two hours, Jarlath and his crew were leaving. Whispering in Zakiya's ear, Jarlath said, "You better be there when I come." Zakiya just looked at him as he walked away, admiring his cockiness.

After Jarlath left, the girls were free to promote without being embarrassed or looking desperate for customers. They began to work the room, telling everybody the updates on the new hot spot.

After all the dancing and networking they did at the club, Zakiya was dying to get back to the room. She took off her new pumps that weren't quite broken in and slid off the dress that now smelled like perfume and cigars. Jumping in the bed, loving the pleasure she was receiving from finally been able to close her eyes.

TIME TO WORK

Zakiya made sure she was the first person up in the morning. Getting dressed didn't even take her as long as it usually did. Her gear was simple, but eye catching. She did right by not wearing bold accessories with the dress. The simple hair and studded pumps let the Chanel dress speak for itself. Today was the grand opening of The Lounge and there were a ton of things that needed to be done.

The moment Zakiya stepped foot outside of the hotel, she got the New York rush. She couldn't believe what was happening. Seeing all the New York traffic moving and her being a part of it was surreal to Zakiya. She still was in love with the way New York operated. It was the smallest things that motivated her, the streets full of cabs, the high fashion billboards, even the homeless. She ran into on the streets. Zakiya arrived at The Lounge and to her surprise, her dedicated workers were there. Saran and Makeeda were already in motion.

"The sign looks great you guys." Zakiya said to Makeeda and Saran. "I think the red color was a great idea."

"Me too," Saran agreed about the large red logo that read LOUNGE.

"Well, we have a lot of work to do girls. So let's get started."

Makeeda and Saran followed Zakiya inside the store. "I want warm colors to bring out the store. Winter will be here before we know it.

Warm colors, coffee, and books, screams a place to come and read, or eat on my lunch break, or after leaving work. I want the books to be organized from gossip magazines to the best newspapers.

I want African American authors in one place, all my romantic novels in another. Look inside the book and see who is the publisher because we are going to sort them out by their publisher. That way my readers won't have a hard time finding what it is they want to read. Also, let's rearrange this furniture a little." Zakiya was turning into a neat freak without trying. But without complaints, Makeeda and Saran did exactly what she wanted them to do.

"Let's set these tables up, Saran, while Makeeda sort the books out." Zakiya demanded. "On top of them should be creamer, sugar, and cream cheese for bagels. Anything else they might need they can ask you when they buy. You are going to work the stand and Makeeda, you work the front. Saran, you think you can handle making the bagels and all kinds of hot chocolate and coffee?"

Saran looks at Zakiya with a rhetorical look written on her face. "Ugh yes, that's nothing. I got it boss lady. No need to worry."

The store was set up nicely. In the front was a nice brown leather sofa set and sofa chairs with autumn colors on top. In the back was the stand where you could order your beverage or bagels. On the second floor you could look down to the first floor; the brown and red Jasper seating booths suited the lounge perfect. The girls were just about finished with everything. All they really had to do was wait for the people to start rolling in. Zakiya wasn't sure how that process would go, but she was very patient. She had a CD that she made off her computer with all kinds of great songs with everybody from Katy Perry and Beyonce, to Lady Anbellum and Lady Gaga. The list was enormous. She wanted to target as many genres as possible because you could hear the music outside the store. The music was doing its job, grabbing people's attention.

"Hey, are you open?" the white lady asked with a cheesy smile.

"Yes we are. Come on in," Makeeda said. Slowly but surely the store was filling up. Some customers browsing books while others were grabbing coffee.

Like a sweet sixteen surprise birthday, Jarlath and over thirty of his friends entered the store. Zakiya was completely caught off guard. She didn't know what to do.

"Hey, do you mind if I hold a meeting here?" Jarlath asked Zakiya. She was stunned.

Some of his biggest employers were standing in her store. She tried her best to shake it off. She couldn't let him see her drool over anyone.

"Of course! Come on in. I will set up a table for you guys in the back."

Makeeda and Saran were working like they already needed a bonus. Before Zakiya could say anything, they were on it. Jarlath pulled Zakiya to the side.

"I don't really have a meeting so they can just entertain themselves. They are going to help support you by buying as many books as possible." Jarlath turned Zakiya towards the large window. "Do you see that?"

Zakiya nodded her head, looking at the paparazzi take pictures. "What are they doing?" Zakiya asked Jarlath in a very surprised tone.

"It's called publicity.

All the New York Times and any magazines for that matter need to know is this celebrity shops here and the business begins to pour in like milk, baby."

Zakiya hugged Jarlath softly. "Thank you, really, but you know I got to ask. Why, and what's in it for you?"

Jarlath cracked a nice charming smile at Zakiya and said, "I hope a date."

"All this to ask me out?"

Very cocky, Jarlath replied, "Well you know I like to be a little different. Besides, I know a young, beautiful girl like you has high standards when it comes to picking a man. And I for one don't accept defeat in no department. So what do you say me, you, and New York for a night?"

Jarlath succeeded, Zakiya was charmed. "Sure, we can take on New York. When are you talking about?"

Jarlath looked at Zakiya, kissed her on the forehead and said, "Tonight. I will be in touch."

Zakiya watched as Jarlath walked out the store thinking, how, when he don't have my number. Jarlath's assistant had paid for some books for him while he and Zakiya talked. He wanted to walk out the store with books, to help promote Zakiya's business. Greeting Jarlath at the door was the paparazzi. Zakiya watched Jarlath until he wasn't visible. She was flattered that he was supporting her. Jarlath left his crew behind.

Some of the underground rappers were having a cup of coffee and some of the supermodels were dancing in the middle of the floor to the music that was playing. Zakiya wasn't sure if Jarlath ordered them to do so, but she was not against any of it. Anything that helped her store out was cool with her. That meant more money and exposure for her. Zakiya felt very lucky. She was getting top of the line publicity in exchange for a date with a very hot and rich guy.

"Makeeda and Saran, close up the store tonight. I'm giving you girls a chance to earn some trust. Be smart." Zakiya said as she walked out the door. "Have fun for the three of us."

The Great Date

Zakiya wasn't sure what to wear. The whole ride back to the hotel had her thinking. She wanted to call and ask, but she didn't have any number to call him on and time was starting to fly by already.

"Shoot he didn't even say when he was coming." Zakiya said to herself quietly in the back of the cab. "I guess I will hurry back to the store with my things and just pack them away when I get back.

"Shoot, but I don't want to get dressed there. I don't have anything ready. Forget it, shoot, I will figure something out. I might just have to pay for another night in the room because rushing is not something I am trying to do. Yeah, I think I will just pay for another day."

The cab driver looked in the mirror at Zakiya as she talked to herself out loud. "$10.17 ma'am."

Zakiya pulled eleven dollars out of her purse and jumped out of the cab trying to beat time. Instead of going straight to the receptionist desk when she walked in, Zakiya decided to call from her room. "Hey how are you doing today?" Zakiya asked the white man on the elevator.

"I'm doing fine and you?"

"Oh, I'm doing fine" Zakiya responded smiling, thinking about her day.

When she walked in her room, a beautiful black cock tail dress laid across her bed. "I can't believe this. I just know he did not buy me a dress. And how the hell did he know where I was staying?"

Zakiya left the dress and the card on the bed waiting to read it. She picked up the room phone and dialed the front desk first. "Hey, this is room 1103, you can just charge the card for one more night."

"Ma'am, your room has already been paid for three more nights. Do you want to pay for another?"

Zakiya was confused, but she didn't want to correct the mistake if there was one. However, she had to make sure her prepaid rush card wasn't charged. "Did the hotel charge my card?"

"No, ma'am. Your fiancée paid for three more nights."

Immediately Zakiya knew who her "fiancée" was. "This man is just full of surprises. Okay that will be all."

Zakiya opened the card, reading, "I will be there to get you at eight. I hope you love the dress as much as I do."

The price tag on the dress read $1,250. "He must have left the price on for me to see it."

Speechless, Zakiya sat on the end of her bed and looked down at the shoes that were out the box seating in front of the dress; they were the most gorgeous black Jimmy Choos. "This man is straight trying to spoil me, I tell you."

The great gifts pushed Zakiya's suspicion about Jarlath to the back of her head. She was no longer wondering how this stranger knew everything about her, from her shoe size, to her dress size or even where she stayed.

αααα

It was eight and finally Zakiya was finished with her hair and make-up. The dress gave Zakiya a classy, but sexy look. She looked nothing like eighteen. This multi-dimensional black gown fully covered and fitted Zakiya's form fabulously.

KNOCK- KNOCK!

"Yes."

The doorman entered Zakiya room. "Your ride is here for you."

Zakiya's palms were sweating. She was very nervous about this date but very anxious. "Okay, I'm right behind you." Zakiya walked behind the doorman who led her to the black Rolls Royce.

"WOW! You look beautiful. Not that I thought you would look anything less."

Zakiya who had nervous written all over her face, said "Thank you" in her very sweet-sounding voice. "So where are we going?"

Jarlath was going to keep Zakiya in suspense but he didn't want to scare her. "To one of my favorite restaurants, this Italian restaurant. Did you want to go somewhere in particular?" Jarlath said, looking in Zakiya's beautiful brown eyes.

"No, I didn't have anything in mind. I just moved to New York, so I don't know too much about the hot spots yet."

Jarlath smiled, showing his beautiful white teeth. "How long have you been here?"

Zakiya was trying to give Jarlath less about her as possible, but Jarlath was smooth and demanding. "Just a couple of weeks."

Jarlath nodded his head. "That's very good. I like your drive. You are very hungry to be so young. How old are you again?" Jarlath asked Zakiya the question she was hoping to avoid. Fortunately for her, the car stopped and the driver opened the door. Only they weren't at an Italian restaurant. Zakiya was amazed. The yacht, siting on the glistening waters, was beautiful. Zakiya stepped out the car confused. She didn't want to lead because she was still confused on where to go.

The view of the city was even more breathtaking.

"Well, aren't you just full of surprises tonight?" Zakiya said to Jarlath as he grabbed her hand, helping her onto the yacht. The yacht had a dinner table set for two with jazz music playing and candles lit. "This is nice, Jarlath. You didn't have to do all of this." Zakiya stated even though she knew she loved the surprises he was giving her and didn't want him to stop.

"I know I didn't have to, but the look on your face is priceless. As I knew it would be."

Zakiya sat down in the chair Jarlath pulled out for her. "So, do you do this for every girl you date?"

Jarlath sat down getting comfortable before answering, "No. However, whenever I do go out, I like to make sure the person I'm taking out is enjoying themselves. I don't date easily. I have been told I'm hard to get. So when I do date, I like to make it worthwhile."

Zakiya couldn't help but think Jarlath was a man who was very sure of himself and wasn't shy about it at all. Zakiya was curious to know how he had so many things at his fingertips, who were his connections and how he was able to get a hold of her. "How did you know where I was staying?" Zakiya asked, sipping on the red wine that was poured into her glass by the server.

"It wasn't hard to find out. This is my city. There's nothing I can't find out here."

"Okay, so how did you know what size dress I wore and the correct shoe size to get?"

Jarlath waved the young Latino boy over to take their order. "You are a ten, butterfly. It wasn't too hard to figure out. Jarlath closed the conversation and order his food. I will have the filled steak and potatoes," Jarlath said to the server.

"Ma'am, are you ready to order?"

"Yes, I will have the pasta salad and roast."

"Sure, will that be all?"

"Yes."

Jarlath stared in the eyes of the beautiful young lady. "You are so beautiful Zakiya, and so is your name."

Zakiya wasn't use to a man being so straight forward with her. She wasn't even used to being with a man. The only person she had ever been with was a boy and he did not make her feel the way Jarlath was making her feel.

"Thank you," Zakiya said with confidence. She remembered her mother telling her to never let a boy or man think that his compliments matter.

That it was alright to thank them as long as he knows that you know how beautiful you are without him telling you. Jarlath noticed Zakiya's confidence.

"You hear that a lot I see." Jarlath asked Zakiya. Politely, but cockily Zakiya responded,

"No. I just don't have to hear it to know I'm beautiful, but like chocolate candy, you can never get enough of it." Jarlath laughed. Laughing was something he didn't do easily, but with Zakiya he felt comfortable enough to be himself and for the first time ever, Zakiya was feeling good off the alcohol.

She had never drank wine before, so after the first two glasses, she was tipsy, yet still in control. Zakiya stood up, grabbing Jarlath's hand. "Come on let's dance." Jarlath stared at Zakiya. He couldn't believe he was thinking about taking her up on the offer.

Jarlath wasn't a dancer and he didn't know how to tell Zakiya that he couldn't dance. For the first time in life, he was shy and uncomfortable. Jarlath stared at the beautiful Zakiya with his legs open, hands placed between them. Trying to ignore Zakiya's offer Jarlath complimented Zakiya on her looks.

"Well, don't you look like a goddess standing in front of me." Jarlath assured Zakiya while allowing her to hypnotize him with her lovely attractive hips and long, thick natural hair that was falling past her shoulders. Jarlath noticed Zakiya's innocence in her exquisite glowing face.

Zakiya ignored the fact that Jarlath was hesitant on dancing. She had already figured that he wasn't the dancing type before asking him. It was the main reason why she wanted to dance with him, for balance. Zakiya was out her comfort zone and she wanted Jarlath to feel the same way.

Besides, she knew the only way to land this man was to take control and to take him to places others were afraid to go.

Zakiya grabbed both of Jarlath's hands and pulled him to his feet. She took his hands and wrapped them around her curvy body, then placed her hands on his large, broad shoulders. Zakiya moved her feet side-to-side slowly to the beat of the nice jazz that was playing, leading the way for Jarlath to follow. She looked the tall, handsome man in the eyes and said, "You said you wanted to show me an amazing time, right?" Laying her head gently on Jarlath's shoulders, she exhaled, inhaling the sweet smell of his Dove for Men soap.

Jarlath like Zakiya, inhaled her delightful smell. The Dolce G Light smelled amazing. Zakiya was scooping Jarlath off his feet with little effort.

The wine had Zakiya feeling like a grown woman. She no longer felt like the young girl from Jackson, Georgia. Jarlath spun Zakiya then dipped her.

"See, you are very good at this."

Jarlath smiled and said, "I don't know how. Dancing wasn't something we did in the hood where I grew up. At least, not this kind of dancing anyway. When I finally made it out of the hood, I never really had an interest in taking a woman dancing." Zakiya smiled.

Jarlath proved her theory right. After dancing for about thirty minutes, Zakiya's and Jarlath's lips met each other. First the kiss was soft, and gentle.

Once Zakiya and Jarlath saw that kiss wasn't satisfying their hormones, they went back in for seconds, coming closer to one another. This kiss was more aggressive. Jarlath took Zakiya's head and held it to his lips thrusting his tongue down her throat.

While his right hand was holding her head to his face, his left hand was massaging her round ass.

Zakiya couldn't fight the hormones that were raising all of sudden. Jarlath's aggressiveness made her hotter than Michael Jackson's Thriller album. Her mind was telling her to make him wait, but her body was screaming for his growing penis to take her to that sinful place. Zakiya was ignoring her mother's voice in her head that was telling her to save herself for marriage.

She allowed Jarlath to sweep her off her feet with no strain, showing strength, he carried her to the master bedroom on the large yacht. Laying Zakiya on the bed, Jarlath trailed her body with wet kisses, licking her navel and continuing on down to her very impatient vagina. He slurped on Zakiya's clitoris like he was sucking a grape popsicle on a hot Atlanta day. Zakiya couldn't fight the feeling Jarlath's amazing head was giving her. Her moans were getting louder. She tilted her head back and arched her body, placing her fat vagina directly in Jarlath's mouth. This was the first time Zakiya ever had oral sex done to her and she was enjoying every bit of it.

After eating Zakiya like a five course meal, Jarlath pulled her body towards his. He left Zakiya's legs wide open, craving her love. It took Jarlath less than three seconds to place the large Trojan on his dick. When Zakiya saw the size of Jarlath's penis, she wanted to take off running, only it was too late for that. Jarlath was unable to put his large head inside of Zakiya the first time so he tried again, attempting to be as gentle as he could.

Jarlath slid his hard dick up and down Zakiya's wet pussy, teasing them both at the same time. Finally, he pushed his dick inside of Zakiya's tight hole.

"OOOHA Jarlath, OOOHA, slow baby, slow!" Zakiya cries for help only hyped Jarlath up more. He thrusted Zakiya's vagina, reaching those never reached spots while still keeping his slow, demanding rhythm.

After easing his way in Jarlath's strokes doubled and Zakiya moans grew louder. She began gripping his broad shoulders, scratching his back with her fake nails.

Jarlath set the mood. The sex was rough and dangerous but compassionate, and Zakiya loved every bit of it. She begin slightly biting Jarlath on his neck, then kissed him softly in the exact spot. She repeated the routine all over his neck, stopping on his chest, sucking it, then kissing it with both lips pressed together. Jarlath held Zakiya close the entire time, continuing to fuck her rough but on beat to the soft R&B music that was playing.

"Damn!" Jarlath whispered to Zakiya

"What?"

Jarlath ignored her question and continued thrusting her vagina. His nut was less than three seconds away and he couldn't pull himself off her. The thought of his nut releasing in her made the semen come faster.

"AHHHA, SHIT Zakiya." Jarlath dropped his weight on Zakiya, kissing her neck in circular motion, then pecking her lips softly and then he went to her cheeks. Jarlath couldn't pull himself together. Zakiya had his hormones by the balls.

"You're amazing," Jarlath whispered to Zakiya after ten minutes of kissing.

Spoiled Intentionally

Jarlath and Zakiya woke up on a private island. The water was clear blue and the weather was warm.

"Jarlath where are we?" Zakiya asked the man who was already awake, sitting on the end of the bed reading The New York Times paper.

"A private island, sweetheart."

Zakiya's heart dropped to her knees. She was not very comfortable being with a man she barely knew on an island she had no knowledge of. "I never knew anything about us coming to an island, Jarlath. I have to get back to the store. You should have asked me before sailing me to the middle of nowhere."

Jarlath continued reading his newspaper showing Zakiya no reaction to her comment. Zakiya watched as Jarlath sat quiet, thinking about those girls on the LifeTime movies. She was always yelling at the TV because of the girls who she thought were being so stupid.

Now she was feeling like them girls, she got herself together and then fixed her tone. She didn't want to upset Jarlath. Especially not right now. She knew nothing about New York or no other place beside Jackson, Georgia. He could do anything to her and no one would know a thing, she thought. "Where are we exactly?" Zakiya asked Jarlath in a calm tone.

"Would you like to go back home?" Jarlath asked, turning around to meet Zakiya's eyes.

"Yes. I had a great time, but I really didn't need to come to a private island. I have like a million things to do. Thank you though. Maybe we can do this another time."

Jarlath couldn't believe his ears. He only asked Zakiya if she wanted to go home because he was sure she would say no. He wasn't used to girls telling him no, it almost never happened. He figured Zakiya was just putting on an act so that she wouldn't seem easy like most of the girls he dated, but when he saw she was dead serious, it brought him to his feet once again. With Zakiya, Jarlath never got a chance to be boring. He constantly had to prove himself and a challenge was something that he rarely turned down.

"Okay, I will take you home, but since we are here I have to pick up some things and then we can be on our way. Cool?"

Zakiya nodded. She had no choice. What else was she going to do, tell the captain to turn the yacht around, as if he would.

Zakiya realized that she wasn't going to be back at the store on time so she picked up the phone and called Saran. "Hey Saran, this is Zakiya."

"I know who you are. Where are you?"

Zakiya took a deep breath then rolled her eyes. "I'm... that's not important. I want you and Makeeda to hold the store down today. I am going to be a little late. Remember good customer service and keep the store clean. Yawl might have to close. I am not for sure. I will call y'all to let you know. If I don't make it before closing time or I don't call before it's closing time, close the store for me. Okay?"

Without thinking it over, Saran said, "Okay, that's no problem. We will do just that, enjoy yourself."

Zakiya hung up on Saran without a bye. She was very irritated at the moment. "How long does it take to get back to New York from here?"

"You won't be back in New York until tomorrow sometime, Zakiya," Jarlath said as he walked out the room, shutting the door behind him.

The yacht stopped so Zakiya slid back on her black cocktail dress after washing down in the bathroom. She didn't know what to think. Her thoughts were all over the place. The LifeTime movies were really messing with her. All the movies with the girls coming up missing after running with guys, just like she was doing. Zakiya didn't know if Jarlath was going to ever take her back to New York. Her hands massaged her temples while she thought about, what stop he had to make? Zakiya had only known Jarlath for a while but she knew he was powerful. She couldn't help but think the stop he had to make was an illegal one. Being this powerful had to require some illegal activities.

"Damn! What the hell I done got myself into? I need to play like I'm sick or something. Let's see, what can I say is wrong with me? Damn, never again, never damn again."

Jarlath walked in the room where Zakiya was pacing the floor talking to herself. "Are you okay?" Jarlath stood firmly, looking Zakiya directly in the eyes.

"Yeah, I am okay. I am just not feeling that good."

"Oh, you might be a little sea sick. Come on with me. A little time off the boat and you will be okay." Jarlath walked out the door and Zakiya felt like crying.

She didn't want to go nowhere but home but she knew she couldn't act suspicious so she went anyway.

Jarlath had a black Escalade waiting for them when the two of them got off the boat. They rode through the most beautiful scenery. There were palm trees and clear blue water everywhere. It was only a handful of houses on the land and they were all big with beautiful, nice cut green grass. Zakiya had never seen a place so beautiful. She kept her face turned to the window. She didn't want to face Jarlath.

After the thirty minute ride, the Escalade had arrived. Zakiya and Jarlath were surrounded by top designers boutique's and retails. If the designer was big, this small town had it. The driver opened the door and Zakiya's heart beats slowed down a little. It was a bittersweet situation. She was still curious, but the destination had calmed her nerves a little. Jarlath hadn't done anything illegal, but Zakiya wasn't counting her chickens yet. Not until they arrived to their final destination.

"What store would you like to shop in?" Jarlath asked standing on the sidewalk, looking around at the surroundings.

"It doesn't matter to me." Zakiya was unsure on how to answer the question. She didn't have any money to spend on clothes so she wasn't going to say a store that was mad expensive.

"Which one do you like?"

"I mean, I like all of them."

"Well let's go to all of them then."

You didn't have to be close to Zakiya to hear the sound of her heartbeats, her heart was racing. In and out of every boutique, Zakiya was showered. You could see her perfect white teeth as she smiled from ear to ear strutting like a million bulks up and down the strip. Zakiya's Hermes Lu Brique Birken bag rested on one arm while her Louis Vuitton and Chanel shopping bags dangled from the other. She never had to look twice at shoes, clothes, expensive bags, jewelry, or shades. Zakiya was balling like rappers do. There was nothing she couldn't buy.

When Zakiya saw the very expensive furniture store, she just had to go in. She was curious. "Excuse me, ma'am," Zakiya said to the pale, thin retailer. "Do y'all do deliveries here?"

"Well, yes we do. Anywhere you want us to."

Those words were like music to Zakiya's ears. She bought the most expensive bedroom and living room sets plus bath decorations for her little apartment. She even bought her two plasma TVs. Jarlath just watched as Zakiya bought everything she desired.

Everything That Glitters Is Not Gold

After a long day of shopping, Zakiya was ready to eat, but she wasn't craving anything expensive. "Let's order some wings from a shack and go to that beautiful park and eat, Jarlath."

Jarlath looked at Zakiya like she was crazy. "Go to what park? And eat what?"

Zakiya laughed, grabbing Jarlath's hand and leading him to the hot wings wagon. "Hey, how are you today?" Zakiya said to the heavy set black lady who looked old enough to be Zakiya's grandma.

"I'm fine and you?"

"I'm great. I will have a ten piece hot, with light lemon pepper sprinkle and a sweet tea. What are you having, Jarlath?"

Jarlath hesitated. "Do I have to eat?"

Zakiya laughed and answered, "Yes, you do."

"Well, I guess I will have the same thing you got and a sweet tea with mine as well."

After writing down the order, the old lady had Jarlath's and Zakiya's food ready in less than six minutes. Jarlath held the food while Zakiya led them to the beautiful waterfall park.

She and Jarlath sat on a bench watching the beautiful waterfall. Dressed in all black, Jarlath's bodyguards stood around them with their hands tucked in their pockets, but Zakiya accepted it. She knew the park was the closest thing to normal she was going to get from Jarlath and after all the splurging she wanted to just chill.

"Why did you want to sit in this park again?" Jarlath was curious about Zakiya's decision. He was a man that believes that every decision had a reason.

"Because I love the view, the sound of the birds chirping, and the peace the silence gives you. Besides, it helps me learn more about the person I'm sharing the beautiful view with. Besides the bodyguards and the money, I know nothing about you. What you like to do for fun? What are you scared of or how many siblings do you have? Do you want kids? Do you have any? You know things like that. The money without character is just no fun. Power without balance can be draining."

Jarlath yet again was amazed with Zakiya's personality. He felt like he was running a marathon without a break. Zakiya kept him on his toes. She wasn't like most girls he dated who were only interested in what he was interested in.

"Well, since we are talking about getting to know each other, you never told me how old you are." Jarlath asked.

Zakiya swallowed her spit hard, so hard that Jarlath could see her throat move while she swallowed her spit. "I'm eighteen. I told you that at the club."

Jarlath couldn't believe what his ears were hearing. He held his head down in his hands while Zakiya laughed. "I forgot you did tell me that. I guess I was hoping you were playing."

Zakiya continued to laugh. "No, I'm not playing. I'm eighteen, I'm very young. Just far from dumb. I was raised a little faster than others. Not by force, but by choice. I have five sisters and am next to the youngest. I just never been my age, what can I say?

I have always been mature. I'm legal, but if I was anything less than legal, I would have told you. So you could have the choice of choosing whether you wanted to date me or not."

Jarlath just listened as the young, but gorgeous girl talked. It was all making sense to Jarlath now. The innocence in Zakiya's face and her very tight vagina.

"I got to say I love that you care about being so much younger than you." Zakiya said with a pleased smile on her face. "It shows a lot about your character. However, I probably can teach your ex-girls a thing or two, age has never stopped my show."

Jarlath laughed shaking his head, speechless. He knew that Zakiya was right about teaching some of his girls a thing or two. She was completely different from the rest. She was almost perfect in his eyes, it was almost hard to accept because she was only eighteen, not that Jarlath didn't date young girls in his days. He just was shocked to find out that Zakiya was a young girl because most of the young girls he had experience with were the complete opposite of Zakiya. She was on a level not even his wife had reached.

"You so young, I bet you can count how many guys you been with," Jarlath wisecracked, not knowing the joke was actually true.

"Yelp, I can and I don't need two hands."

The fact that Zakiya could count on her hands how many guys she had been with made Jarlath want her more. Zakiya was now worth more in his eyes. "Well, I have no problem with that. I love that you are limited edition. Not too many guys can say they have had you and that suits me well. I like what the next man can't get or never had. It just took me by surprise because you act as if you are my age."

"Which I didn't catch by the way," Zakiya said biting into her hot wing.

"You didn't catch it because I didn't throw it. Jarlath dipped his fries in his blue cheese. You might choke if I told you. Just know I'm old enough to be your daddy." He stated before chopping down his fries.

Zakiya smiled watching Jarlath eat his food. "I thought I was the only one who ate my fries like that." After washing her food down with the ice cold sweet tea Zakiya jumped back to the subject. "And that doesn't surprise me."

"Oh you got jokes I see." Jarlath wasn't lost at all on Zakiya's age joke.

The two sat quietly, listening to the birds chirp while they finished their food and right after they finished Zakiya and Jarlath walked back to the SUV. "I really enjoyed myself Jarlath, even though you made me miss a day at the store. Next time warn a sistah. You know the surprise trips and thangs like that."

"If I warned a sistah then it wouldn't be a surprise, now would it? I get your point though. I will make it up to you, I promise. Since we are telling each other things about one another, there's something I need to tell you about me."

The feeling was back just like that. It was like Zakiya had to hold her breath and pray for good news. She never knew what to expect with him. Her heart began to race again and her palms were sweaty. Once again her thoughts were running all over the place. Zakiya sat up on the suede seats in the Escalade, ears wide open, fully alert, giving Jarlath all of her attention. "What is it, Jarlath? I'm listening."

Jarlath sat silent for a while longer thinking about if he should tell her. He knew once he spilled to her his news, she would never look at him the same. "I will tell you if you promise not to be judgmental right off the back. The situation may seem a little too much

122

to take, but just remember this when I tell you. It's only temporary." Zakiya repeated Jarlath's last sentence in her head. Its only temporary, It's only temporary, It's only temporary, trying to figure out what it could be.

Zakiya was running out of time, the truck had arrived at the yacht. The two jumped out of the car with silence between them and as soon as they were inside the boat Zakiya turned to Jarlath and nodded her head "yes, I'll keep that in mind." She would tell Jarlath anything to hear what he had to say. "Dammit Jarlath, what is it?" Zakiya was about to explode. Her thoughts were full and her patience was low.

"I'm married Zakiya."

Zakiya shook her head even though she was slightly relieved, knowing that the news could have been worse "Damn Jarlath, you got me having sex with you and shit. I don't believe in that type of junk. Seriously, like why you are here with me if you are married and shit? One girl is not enough for you? What kind of man cheats on his wife anyway?"

Zakiya never allowed Jarlath to answer any of her questions. She answered them and rambled on with more, "a kind who don't give a damn, that kind. Well, it was fun while it lasted. I knew it was something. It's that Alayne girl, right? Yeah, that's who it probably is. I saw you come to the party with her that night. I just didn't think you would be so rude and flirt with me if she was any kind of spouse to you. Yelp that damn cocky shit thrown me all the way off that time."

Zakiya was pacing the floor, going on and on she didn't even recognize Jarlath silence. He sat on the bed with the most dangerous face. He cared for Zakiya and that wasn't easy for him to do. All he wanted to do was tell her the truth so that she wouldn't leave him in the future for not telling her.

Once he realized that he was going to lose her anyway, his heart began pounding in a way he didn't agree with. The thought of not having Zakiya made him furious. He felt trapped. He didn't know what to say to convince her that the marriage could be over with a blink of an eye. So he just said it, giving it a try. "My marriage is over. I will be divorced before you know it. Now sit down and stop getting yourself all worked up about nothing."

Zakiya stood between Jarlath's legs, pushing his shoulders. "Worked up about nothing?" she asked, turning his statement into a question. "I just slept with a married man, Jarlath. Damn Makeeda said that you were married but I figured she was just saying that so I wouldn't talk to you."

"You just slept with a separated man, Zakiya and she only knows what the media tells her."

"Well, hell, it's all the same."

"No, it's not. That's why it's called separation. It's what you do when you are minutes away from a divorce."

"Do you think that I am going to sit around and play your mistress? Why you feed me with a plateful of lies on how you are going to get a divorce? It just takes time, or I got a lot on my plate, don't question me about my wife Bullshit! Zakiya said throwing her hands up in the air.

"Or the most famous one, I just can't do her like that." Zakiya hands were on her hips and head and eyes was rolling as she spit out her thoughts loudly to Jarlath. She knew a married man had nothing to offer a single woman and she wanted him to know she knew. "Who in their right mind will allow themselves to grow feelings for a married man? Especially when you know he is married. That's like suicide. I'm not trying to hurt myself, Jarlath. But I tell you one thing. I do thank you for being honest with me. That tells me a lot about your character. You could have kept quiet and you didn't, so thank you. But I can't do it, Jarlath, I'm sorry. I like you too much. The feelings will come full speed and I can't take that chance."

For the first time, Jarlath felt helpless. He couldn't control the situation. He so badly wanted to pour his feelings out like a cold glass of champagne but he didn't want to risk them getting hurt, so he passed. "If that's what you want then so be it and you are not welcome by the way. I tell you the truth and you treat me like some damn dog off the streets, like I'm out to bite you or something. You never, not once, allowed me the time to plead my case. So good luck and no worries, you will never have to worry about me ever. I'm gone with the wind, baby girl.

Revenge

"I really enjoyed myself today. The food was great."

Jarlath ignored the tall, slim girl with the Brooklyn accent.

"Do you need me to do anything for you before I take a bath?"

Jarlath flipped through the channels continuing to ignore the beautiful girl.

"Well, I'm going to take a bath. If you need anything just call me." The long legged girl walked in the bathroom and took a long look in the mirror.

"What are you doing? Get it together, don't blow this. Shit, who am I fooling? This nigga is not stunned by me at the least. He won't even look at me. Pull it together, think, think. What do all niggas love and no nigga can say no to? Duh, great head and good sex, yeah that's it."

The beautiful girl took a shower, cleaning harder than usual. "When he goes down here, I don't want him to smell nothing but water and soap, baby."

She continued talking to herself humming a soft tone, confident about her new plan for wheeling Jarlath in.

"Damn, I wish I had an ovulation test and some yeast cream. I would trap his fine ass. That's alright, once I finish with his ass, he going to want me without the extra force and constant reminders."

After having a long conversation with herself, the girl walked out of the restroom, towards Jarlath. She kneeled down on the floor, her legs glistening from the shower, and spread his legs apart. Jarlath knew what was coming the moment she kneeled before him.

He never had to ask. They just gave. Whenever he deliberately ignored them, they would go to sex for a response, the same routine, different girl. That's why Zakiya was so special to him. He never was bored with her. She was smart, beautiful, and very charming. She didn't pretend to be anyone but herself and she always put herself before him. Jarlath took one glance down at the girl and shook his head, he wiped his face hoping it would wipe his thoughts of Zakiya away but it didn't. It just made him think about her more. He wanted to tell the girl to leave but he couldn't, he had to teach Zakiya a lesson.

The girl thought that Jarlath would be extra excited about getting what she was about to offer him, but instead he watched her with lack of excitement and arrogance on his face. Jarlath was still flipping through the channels on the TV when the Brooklyn beauty took a handful of his grown dick, massaging it, taking as much as she could in her mouth, and gulping it in and out.

Jarlath took his free hand and took the girl's head, shoving his dick entirely in her mouth, ignoring the fact that she was slightly choking. She wanted so bad to please him she continued sucking the dick to her jaws was norm. The moment Jarlath's nut started to release, he took his penis out her mouth, Squirting the release all over her face and hair.

"You can stay in the room. Check out time isn't until 12:00 p.m." Jarlath took a wet rag from the bathroom and washed his penis before leaving. He was even more angry than before but he was looking forward to Zakiya's reaction. Jarlath would do anything to get Zakiya's attention, he was missing her like crazy but he wasn't by himself

It had only been two weeks since Zakiya spoke to Jarlath and she was already missing him. Even though she knew letting Jarlath go was the right thing to do, she still yearned for his company, his touch, and his charms.

"OOH, somebody got some flowers coming in," Saran said, looking at the delivery guy with a handful of flowers.

Zakiya thought to herself, I knew he was missing me just as much as I was missing him.

"Dang, Miss Zakiya what you do to this man. Got him bringing you flowers and everything," Makeeda said as the man set the flowers on the glass counter. "Which reminds me, you never told us about your date, Zakiya. I thought we were cool enough to at least get high off your supply." Saran added looking at Zakiya with her hands on her hips.

Zakiya ignored Saran as she read the flowers that were sent to Makeeda from Jarlath. Her heart was at a standstill. She could hardly breathe. Her blood began to warm up as her hands started to shake. This was the ultimate betrayal. Even though Zakiya knew that Jarlath was only trying to get back at her, the pain still numbed her like a Vicodin. Zakiya ripped the card until the pieces were too small to rip.

"Hey how are you doing today?" Zakiya asked the young lady in the checkout line.

"Do you like flowers, ma'am?"

"Well, yes I do especially when they Saffron Crocus" the thick sister said to Zakiya in her sweet toned voice.

"Well today is your lucky day." Zakiya gave the lady the flowers while Makeeda packed her Essence Magazines in her bag. "Have a nice day."

"I will. Y'all do the same here."

Saran was confused while Makeeda was curious. Zakiya took one long look at Makeeda, giving her the eye that kills and from that one look Zakiya got the answer she needed from Makeeda. She looked like she could shit out teardrops.

From that moment on, Zakiya knew that this wasn't the first encounter Makeeda and Jarlath had. Zakiya whispered in Makeeda's ear loudly; "he is only using you to hurt me. You is so not his type at all. You don't know what you are playing with sweetie, but don't worry, I'm not the one to hate. So like the players of the game would do, I congratulate you on your new disaster. Girl. Once he's finished dogging you, you won't have a voice to bark with. Oh yeah, when he sees that having you on his side doesn't bother me, he is going to let you loose. So when you see him, please let him know that Zakiya wishes him all the luck in the world. Life goes on, shit, it never stopped. Not for him or for no one."

Saran tooted her nose up to Makeeda's stinky betrayal. "How could you, Makeeda? Saran asked shaking her head side-to-side, rolling her eyes in disgust. You know that man don't care shit about you. Not even a little bit. He could care less if you die or live.

That's so trifling." Makeeda rolled her eyes. "Y'all don't know shit about me, okay. I'm from...."

Before Makeeda could get her town out, Zakiya and Saran finished it for her. "Brooklyn, we know."

Makeeda rolled her eyes even harder. "Well, act like it then. I know everything there is to know about this man. Shit, y'all just learning about him, so don't try and tell me shit about him. I know everything there is to know."

"You know what you hear stupid, but you don't know shit about him personally. Hell his own family, close friends, and wife don't even know him." Zakiya assured Makeeda.

Makeeda just watched and listened as Saran and Zakiya drilled her. On the inside, she knew they were right, but she wasn't going to show them. Besides, Makeeda wasn't ready to give up on what her and Jarlath was sharing even if it was little to nothing. She felt like she was closer to becoming someone being with him. In her mind he was only shy and had to come around.

"Well, you don't have to worry about coming back tomorrow. After today, your services here are no longer needed. I can't trust you around my money. I don't know what other snake moves you got up your sleeves. Going out with Jarlath probably would have been alright if you could have done it the right way. I just can't have any sneaky people around me. I am trying to build a business here and I don't need the negativity. So you can leave now. Here is your money I owe you. Just sign this receipt and you can be on your way."

Makeeda's eyes were wet. A part of her wanted to cry but most of her was relieved. She now had a reason to call Jarlath and lean on him for support. She was anxious to make up for the night before. Makeeda knew in her mind the flowers meant he was ready to take it to the next level.

αααα

"Yo?" Jarlath said as he answered the phone.

"Hey Jarlath, this is Makeeda. What you doing?"

Jarlath looked at his phone twice checking the number on it. "Hey, did you get the flowers I sent you?"

Makeeda quickly answered, "Yes, they were beautiful even though I didn't get to keep them."

"Why what happened?"

"Your little friend gave them away to a customer and shredded the card. Oh yeah, she told me to tell you good luck with your life. She wishes you the best. She thinks that you and I are a front and that we will never last. I assured her differently, but the bitch just thinks she knows it all."

Jarlath listened to Makeeda talk. He couldn't help but smile. Zakiya was a tough cookie and giving the flowers away to a customer was a sweet move.

"Oh yeah, she fired me. She claimed it's not because I'm with you but because she don't need any snakes around her. That I'm not trustworthy. She says she would have kept me around if I wasn't so sneaky. I don't believe her. I think she is hurt and just using her business as an excuse to fire me." I should have known it wouldn't work. Jarlath thought to himself while Makeeda rambled on.

Unfortunately for Jarlath, he believed Zakiya only because he was the same way. He would have loved to make her more jealous than she showed or for her to show that she cared. He didn't allow people he didn't trust in his circle, so he completely understood her. That was another reason why he was so attracted to Zakiya because she was strictly about business and if she was ever hurt, like Jarlath, you would never know.

At that moment, Jarlath knew it wasn't going to be easy to have Zakiya as his or even hurt her for that matter. The whole process was going to be a challenge and he couldn't back out of a challenge because it wasn't in his nature. Plus the more battles he lost with Zakiya, the more he wanted her on his team.

"Don't worry about your job. I will have you working in no time. And don't call me, I will call you."

Jarlath hung up the phone and Makeeda screamed at the top of her lungs. The cab driver watched her through his mirror, laughing.

"I'm on my way up! Shit, who knows I might even get a husband out the deal!" Makeeda yelled.

A GOOD NIGHT

"Hey Saran, how are you doing?"

"I'm fine Zakiya. Is everything alright?"

" Yea, I'm fine. I'm just bored. I was wondering would you like to go to the Christian Cota's first Mercedes Benz Fashion Week show? You know its fashion week here in New York and I just wanted to get out and enjoy myself."

Saran was never excited about New York fashion week. She was never financially stable to enjoy it. "Um, I don't know. Fashion and me are not real cool like that."

"Oh don't worry about that, girl. We can go shopping."

Saran remained quiet until Zakiya said, "On me."

"Okay, why not. I will meet you at the store in about ten minutes. I am not that far away." "Okay, cool."

Zakiya easily snuck her ten thousand off Jarlath's card making Jarlath believe that the store only took cash, she pretend to be shopping but she pocketed the money instead. Plus, her store was doing great because of Jarlath's marketing idea. So there was no reason for Zakiya to allow Jarlath to spoil her good spirit.

"Hey, are you in there?" Saran yelled in the hallway of Zakiya's upstairs apartment.

"Yeah, I'm here, stop screaming girl and come on in."

"Wow! This place looks nice. The furniture is amazing and you got style. Who would have ever thought?"

"Whatever honey, you know style is my middle name."

"Yeah, you right about that. You love anything that requires large amounts of green presidents." Saran set on Zakiya's black and gray sectional sofa. "So guess what I find out today?"

Zakiya's stomach instantly caught butterflies. She always got butterflies when she was about to hear bad news.

"I wasn't going to tell you today but I think you should know."

"What is it already Saran?"

"Jarlath opened Makeeda a shoe store across the street from us. You know that empty retail space that's been there for a while?"

"Yeah, the one I was talking about getting to open me a shoe store. Yeah, I know which one you talking about but you know what? I'm not going to give him the benefit of the doubt. Thank you for telling me though."

"Always honey. I just think what you doing at your age is great and I'm not the one for the trifling moves myself. You know all that sneaky shit. That's why when I introduced you to her, I said my associate. She has no friends. Her own family don't even mess with her. She has been blowing my phone up talking about how she's sorry and I knew her first. She even asked me to work for her. Which you will never have to worry about me doing that."

"Well, I just want you to know, I will not be mad at you if you decided to work for Makeeda. I mean you have known her far longer than me, but I would like for you to put in a two week notice. This is a business so you are going to have employees who come and go, so what, life goes on." Zakiya threw her hands up in the air before attempting to walk off.

"Girl, you are not hearing me." Saran stated to Zakiya pointing to her ear. "I do not want to work for her, and between me and you, I hear he is dogging her. It's not even what it seems at all."

"Oh you don't have to tell me. They were never fooling me baby, believe that but anyway, enough of that. I got us front row tickets to the fashion show. So we got to be on point, honey. I got some dresses in the closet with the tags still on and shoes or would you prefer going to the store?"

"I don't mind shopping in your closet. What you got in there that will make me pop?"

Without thinking, Zakiya pulled out the Basil Soda strapless mini with silver detailing and some Nicholas Kirkwood heels. "Yes, girl you know your fashion. For the first time, I'm going to be able to enjoy fashion week." Saran added.

"You never participated in New York's fashion week, Saran?" Zakiya asked with her hands on her hips.

"No honey, I run and hide somewhere."

Zakiya burst out laughing at Saran. "Well let's go have some fun, honey." Zakiya twirled in the mirror.

Dressed in a Mark Fast all black cut-out dress that could stop traffic and cause a serious accident, along with her multi-colored Christian Louboutin Futura Booties. "Damn, I'm one hot girl," Zakiya said, looking in the mirror at her great form. "Are you ready to give New York some action tonight, Saran?"

Saran wasn't sure how to answer the question. She never saw Zakiya in a partying state. She was always professional and strictly about business. "Yeah, let's do it. We smell good, look great, and we young. I don't see anything stopping us."

The girls arrived at the fashion show and it was like a live magazine, Zakiya couldn't get enough of the different designers. After Zakiya and Saran finished walking around the fashion show they decided to take their seats. To their surprise, Jarlath was sitting in the seat next to the one Zakiya and Saran bought.

"OMG! I don't even believe this shit! I know he is not sitting in the seat next to mine out of all the damn seats in this damn fashion show." Zakiya rolled her hazel colored eyes, resting her hands on her hips looking at the seat for about five minutes before deciding to take a seat.

"Just breathe Zakiya, remember a night of fun. BREATHE. DON'T LET HIM SPOIL YOUR NIGHT! Hell, instead spoil his."

Zakiya's high cheeks and deep dimples let Saran know that Zakiya agreed with the idea, her smile was to die for. "You know what Saran. That's the best damn advice you have ever given. Hell, I can't even believe you giving me advice at all."

Zakiya and Saran walked to their seats looking at Jarlath and Alayne sitting in their seats next to the one Zakiya reserved for them. Zakiya strutted right past Alayne and sat next to Jarlath, looking breathtaking.

"I love them Louboutin, girl. You are working them honey," Alayne said to Zakiya as she walked past in the booties that were made of suede and patent leather material and featured a 6 inch white colored heel.

"Oh thank you, beautiful." Zakiya sat in her seat smiling at Jarlath who was damn near drooling and Saran joined her, seating in the seat left of her. Zakiya crossed her feet's at the ankle, resting her hands in her lap.

"So how is that divorce going?" Zakiya asked Jarlath who was staring.

"It's coming along. Why, are you waiting?"

"Not in a million years, but congratulations."

Alayne was into the fashion show that was starting and wasn't paying any attention to Jarlath's and Zakiya's conversation.

"You look stunning, Zakiya. I'm glad to see you."

Zakiya tooted her lips and crossed her long shiny toned legs, saying, "I know" leaving Jarlath with his compliment in his hand and no thank you to wash it down with.

Saran was so excited to see all the A-list celebrities that she tuned Zakiya's and Jarlath's cocky conversation out, giving all her attention to the runway. Everybody from Eve to Kelly Rowland, to Kanye West was there. The fashion show was great, for the first time Saran got to see the fashion before it was out of style and Alayne couldn't take her eyes off all the new competition that walked the runway.

Zakiya asked to take a picture with Alayne then she asked Jarlath to join while Alayne took the picture. Jarlath was confused about Zakiya's decision on taking a picture, but he knew it was part of some strategy of hers. He went along with her, curious and anxious to see what the reasoned was.

Zakiya and Saran stopped by a Manhattan bar after the fashion show and had a couple of Sour Apple Martinis that Saran had to purchase. The girls were wasted, messing with every guy they had seen were single, even the ones who had dates. New York was beautiful at night. The tall buildings and moist streets were great. Zakiya and Saran walked the streets while inhaling the New York midnight air.

Jarlath: Tired Of Lonely

The ride on the way home was silent. Neither Jarlath nor Alayne spoke to one another. They both looked out the window closer to them thinking the whole ride home, look at him over their trying not to look at me. Alayne cut her eyes at Jarlath while his head was turned. I wonder if its hope for our marriage, Lord knows I can't afford to lose both him and Kilo. Alayne turned her head back towards the window and rubbed her hands threw her hair, calming her nerves. Meanwhile, Jarlath was thinking, Damn Zakiya looked good tonight. I got to have her. The woman that's carrying my name is not doing the job for me. I'm tired of lonely and she is not filling the void.

Jarlath cellular phone started to vibrate in his pocket, breaking his thought process. "Hello."

"Can you talk?" Lisa asked Jarlath.

"Yeah, what's up?" "I was calling to tell you about a conversation I overheard your wife having on the phone." Jarlath could tell by the seriousness in Lisa voice that the news was juicy. He looked over at Alayne and said "Yeah, what was it?" Lisa paused for second not knowing how to start the conversation.

"Hello, you there?" Jarlath asked Lisa who was breathing heavily in the phone.

"Yeah, I'm here." Lisa couldn't find an easy way to spill the beans, so she just came right out and said it. "I overheard Alayne talking to Kilo's girlfriend on the phone and she told Alayne that a witness, I mean well her private investigator saw Kilo get pulled over by a policeman in Central Park. Lisa caught her breath. She wrapped the news up in three minutes, ready to get off the phone with Jarlath. It didn't seem that hard to say rehearsing in the restroom. Jarlath took one last look at Alayne and thought, I just can't trust her with my eyes open. Betrayal after betrayal. that's fine, I'll get the last laugh.

"I'm not going to ask you how you heard, just know if you ever hear anything pertaining to me, it will be the last thing you hear." CLICK. Soon after Jarlath hung up the phone he pressed speed dial number five and on the second ring his right; hand worker answered.

"Yo." "I got some leads I need you to look into. Meet me at the office tomorrow and beat me there." Jarlath's phone lit up after he pressed the end button. Less than ten minutes after hanging up the phone, Jarlath's Maybach pulled up to his home. The home Jarlath dreaded coming home to. To him there was no life in the house. Jarlath shook his head getting out the car, trying to get Zakiya off his mind. He knew it wasn't the right time to pursue her, but soon he was going to make her his.

PERFECT 10

Zakiya wasn't feeling good the day after the fashion show, so she let Saran run the store. With the new employees she hired, someone more experienced had to be around to train them. She couldn't stay out of the bathroom. Every five minutes, she was throwing up. "I promise I will never drink again." Zakiya could barely stand up on her two feet. She tried every remedy she could think of and none of them worked.

She decided to swallow her pride and call her mother who she hadn't spoken to in almost a month. Zakiya knew that her mother was going to be extra nosey. Picking up the black and silver cordless phone, she held down her mother's speed dial, 5.

After the second ring, Mary answered the phone, "Hey Zakiya, are you okay? Is everything all right?"

"Momma I'm fine, calm down, calm down, I was just calling to see how you were doing?"

"I'm fine now that I can hear your voice, you almost never call Zakiya. I know you are trying to find yourself, but I am still your mother and I worry about you sometimes baby."

"I know Momma, and I will be more considerate from now on, but trust me, it was never done intentionally. I just been so caught up with running the store, I haven't really had time."

"So how is your store going, Zakiya?"

"Oh it's doing great, Momma. I wish you and my sisters could come up here. I mean, the store is doing great. I'm doing great. Like I'm living my dream, Momma, and I have completed my first book as well. I mean like I'm so ready for the success I know am destined for. It's like I can smell it." Zakiya was so enthusiastic.

Mary's heart was warm and her smile was wide. "Well I can see that you are happy and that makes me happy. I got to say I am proud of you. You sound like one of them career oriented young ladies and I can tell you have matured heavily. I just wish you the best baby and ask that you don't be a stranger. All you girls are branching out now. Melody has moved in with Micah and Layla and Troy have moved to Atlanta. Troy was offered a job with UPS. Cambria and Harley have moved to New Jersey."

Zakiya was surprised to know that her sister was so close. "Momma, I didn't know that Cambria and Harley was staying in New Jersey. That's not too far from me. I can visit them."

"You would know if you called more often and when do you plan on coming to visit me? I hope you are coming down for the holidays."

Zakiya laid back, hoping the nausea would go away. She wasn't planning on coming home for the holidays. The holidays were one of the things that made her crave New York. She had always wanted to participate in New York's holiday festivities, specially Rockefeller Center was one of them. "I don't know, but wouldn't it be great if y'all came to New York? I mean, I will be more than happy to pay for the tickets."

"Now where will you get that kind of money from Zakiya? Plus you know Grandma Annabella is not about to get on no plane. But we will talk about that later. Blend some carrots, orange juice, pepper, and celery to get rid of that hangover, young lady."

Zakiya burst out laughing. "Oh, you so great, how did you know I was hungover, Momma?"

"Girl I was once young not to mention you have a dozen sisters before you."

"Momma, can you call back and leave Cambria's number on my answer machine. I want to call her when I get better."

"Yeah, I can. Go drink that juice and have yourself another beer."

"Okay Momma, bye."

αααα

"Well don't you look like a breath of fresh air this morning." Saran said to Zakiya as she watched Zakiya walk in the store with a new pep in her walk.

"What are you so happy about today, Ms. Thing?" Zakiya asked Saran.

"Well for starters, I saw your best friend over there crying. I think she got the picture with you and Mr. Jarlath on it."

Zakiya burst out laughing. "Oh, how strange. I wonder how that happened?"

"Me too."

"Wow! Look at that sunshine walking this way. He is fineeeeee. Damn!" Saran said licking her lips.

"Oh my God. He is cute." Zakiya said.

"Put on your best smile, Zakiya, you are about to meet your future husband."

"Saran, girl, I am not looking for no husband. Not right now anyway," Zakiya said with her back turned from the register.

"And why aren't you? A lady with your beauty should already be taken." The guy with the smooth baritone stated.

Zakiya was speechless and very hesitant to turn around and face the stranger with the charming compliments.

"Beauty alone is not enough to guarantee a blissful healthy marriage. Zakiya responded. "You have to have trust, smarts, charm, and a hellavu personality, some times more than that. My name is Zakiya and yours?"

"I'm Detective Khalon. And that's a beautiful name you have."

"Thank you. Yours is not so normal itself."

"So when is your next break? Maybe we can sit down and have some coffee together."

Saran was desperate to join in the conversation. "Oh, she doesn't have to wait for a break. She owns the place."

Khalon smiled, showing his perfect white teeth. "Is that right? That means you can't make up an excuse."

"Not that I would because if I didn't want to have a sit down, I will just say it."

"I see you are a very cocky chick. What part of New York you from?"

Zakiya gave Khalon a smirk while leading him to a table in the back. Saran smiled and trailed behind them to take their order and to be nosey. For the first time since Jarlath, Zakiya was speaking to a man and Saran wanted front row to the conversation. Before sitting down at the booth, Zakiya corrected Khalon.

"I'm not from New York. I'm from Georgia." Zakiya blushed at her cockiness then turned towards

Saran to order her favorite coffee. "Black with ten creams and twenty sugars and a cheese cream bagel."

"I see you like your sugar."

"Yeah, I have to taste it in my coffee or else I won't drink it, but enough about me. Where are you from?"

"I'm from Brooklyn."

Zakiya sipped her black coffee. "Everybody I meet is from Brooklyn. That is like the second most popular place here in New York."

"And what is the first one?"

"Manhattan."

Khalon laughed hard. "Yeah, I see you fresh. You still got peaches on the tongue."

Zakiya smiled, raising her left eyebrow, giving Khalon eye-to-eye contact. "And what is that supposed to mean?"

"You got a lot to learn about New York. If you don't mind, I would like to take you out one of these days somewhere, anywhere. What haven't you seen yet in New York?"

Zakiya continued sipping on her coffee, thinking about where she would like to go. "Well, I haven't been anywhere really, so surprise me. It's your town."

"That's no problem, I can do that. Where can I come and get you?"

"Here at the store. It's where I spend most of my hours, if not all of them."

"Trust me, I understand. I will come around eight so look out for me. As a matter of fact, give me your number."

Zakiya dialed her number in Khalon's Blackberry, humming along with Adele's Someone Like You.

"Oh another thing," Zaikya snapped her finger. "I need to know what to wear." She pointed her index finger to Khalon. "So once you figure out where you taking me, call me or text me what you think I should wear."

Khalon took a good look at Zakiya up and down. "That body will make anything look good, but I will call you or text you, that's no problem."

Zakiya twirled her long hair between her fingers, blushing. "I will see you tomorrow then."

As soon as Khalon walked out the door, Zakiya and Saran start screaming, forgetting all about the customers who were just watching them in the store.

"OMG! He is so fine, Zakiya, and you know me. I had to do a little research on him. You know, find out where I know that familiar face from. So I googled him and guess what I found out?"

"What girl?"

"That he is one of New York's best detectives. So finally you can be on the good side of the law. If you know what I mean."

Saran and Zakiya started to laugh again.

"I'm sorry ma'am, can I help you?" Zakiya turned towards the customer who seemed to be having difficulties finding what she was looking for.

"No that's okay. I found what I'm looking for."

Zakiya went back to smiling after the customer assured her that she was fine.

    *   *   *   *

"You can wear the sexiest thing in your closet," Khalon texted Zakiya. Zakiya didn't understand why she was smiling so much. She wasn't even looking for a man or a date. She was enjoying being a single girl in New York, but this guy had her feeling like she was flying. It was a must that she to dress to kill. Zakiya was going to make sure that

Khalon remembered this night if he didn't remember anything else.

αααα

Dressed to kill, Zakiya was a glam goddess in a fully embellished Emilio Pucci mini, paired with a matching clutch and Christian Louboutin spike heels.

She had kept Khalon waiting for about twenty minutes and he wasn't complaining. Mouth semi-wide, Khalon fixated on Zakiya for a long sixty seconds before he could murmur the word, "Wow! You look stunning. Not that I thought you would look anything less."

Zakiya blushed and you could see her high cheeks and deep dimples. "Thank you."

Khalon took Zakiya's hand and they both walked out to his all black Range Rover. Zakiya couldn't help but think this man was the one for her. He was no Jarlath, but he seemed to be an honest, well-rounded man with goals, who actually worked for his accomplishments. Someone she could enjoy the night with, without worrying if they were going to run across doing something illegal. Her heart was beating for a completely different reason. The passion between the two was heated. Khalon didn't want to try and surprise Zakiya and get surprised. He thought, you just never know what girls like these days. So he decided to tell Zakiya about their plans for the night.

"New York fashion week winds down today and celebs have been making their rounds to get in on the last few moments of action at the Lincoln Center. From your very expensive look, I can tell you have a huge appetite for fashion. So what better way to get a preview of what they'll be wearing next fall? I got us front row seats. The coveted front row is just as much as a show as the designs on the runway. Would you like that?"

Zakiya was still smiling uncontrollably. "Yeah, I will love to go." It was going to be Zakiya's second fashion show and she loved it. Zakiya was doing everything she dreamed about doing in New York. A life was only getting better. Lights, camera, and action were three words to describe Zakiya's new life style. Red carpet after red carpet, everybody who was somebody was pulling up, splurging in front of the cameras.

"Oh my goodness, is that Sarah Jessica Parker? I have to ask her for a picture. Will that embarrass you?" Zakiya turned to Khalon who was driving and asked.

Khalon gave Zakiya a sexy laugh. "Of course not, go ahead. I will take the picture if she says yes."

Once the truck came to a complete stop Zakiya jumped out, walking up to the Sex in the City star as calmly as she could. Khalon trailed her after giving his keys to valet. "Hey Sarah, I don't mean to bother you, but I'm like your biggest fan. You are one of the main reasons I moved to New York. Can I get a picture with you?" Zakiya smiled hoping to get a yes.

Sarah was flattered. With a huge smile, she responded, "Yes, I would love to."

Khalon took the picture in Zakiya's Blackberry. "Thank you for your time." Zakiya said.

"No problem and I love the shoes you are wearing." Zakiya was flattered and very confident about her gear. "Thank you, I don't need to say anything about the killers you are wearing. They speak for themselves."

Sarah gave Zakiya a long laugh.

"If you are not a tourist, I don't know what you are." Khalon joked with Zakiya as they walked away from Sarah.

"I know, but I love her so you're just gonna have to be that guy who brought that country girl with him to the fashion show tonight." Zakiya laughed at her own joke and Khalon joined. The two laughed about everything. They even made side jokes about the supermodels who ripped the runway looking too serious. The fashion show brought them closer.

After seeing some of New York's finest celebrities, Khalon decided to take Zakiya to his very own Brothers Spaghetti. The restaurant was known for some of the best cooked spaghetti in New York. The different varieties of sauces and techniques of cooking the spaghetti was the reason for its success. Khalon directed Zakiya in the kitchen where a table for two was set up with candles and an expensive bottle of grape wine on ice.

"This is beautiful. Who would have ever thought you had a romantic side."

"Girl, please, this is only the beginning." Khalon prepared his favorite dish for Zakiya, baked cheese and mushroom spaghetti with cheesy garlic bread and fried corn for sides.

"This food looks amazing. Who taught you how to cook?"

"I was forced to learn. I didn't have anyone to do it for me. I looked after my younger sister. So, she and I took turns cooking for each other."

Zakiya closed her eyes, bowed her head, and said her grace. Khalon was shocked a girl so young had such good manners.

After saying grace Zakiya asked Khalon, "do you rent out restaurants for all your dates?"

Khalon swallowed down his spaghetti with some of the cold grape wine. "No, I haven't been on a date in months. But I don't have to rent out the restaurant because I own it."

Zakiya wanted to reach down to pick her face up off the floor. "Oh, this is a great restaurant you have. You must be real busy between being a detective and running a restaurant too."

"I also have a club to run, but no, I don't. I'm very good with consuming time."

"So, why are you single? You can cook, very career oriented, and you are a good looking man."

Khalon blushed. "Well thank you. I didn't know you were so fond of me, but I lost my wife if you are really interested, and I haven't really been into dating like that since."

Zakiya did it again. She put her foot in her mouth again. "Sorry, I didn't know."

"No need to apologize, its fine. She passed after a bad car wreck. I think it was best because she would have only been suffering if she lived. Out of respect for her, I decided to give her body time to get cold before I went out and got me another spouse."

"I so understand. I think that is very respectful as well. In fact you look even more beautiful now than you did ten minutes ago."

Khalon continued to blush. "I see you are good with words."

"Yeah, it becomes easy to do when there is great inspiration." Before parting ways, the two shared a soft, simple but memorable kiss.

After a lovely night with Khalon, Zakiya went back to her diva pad alone, relaxing in some expensive bubble bath, listening to an R&B old school classic CD she bought off of the TV. The CD had everybody from Gerald Levert to Luther, to Johnny Gill, Keith Sweat, and R Kelly.

After Zakiya's long bath, she was hungry again. She didn't understand why, since she had just eaten less than an hour ago. She went to the kitchen to grab some hot Cheetos and a kosher pickle, then went back to her sofa that was close to the window with the beautiful view of Manhattan.

THE CHASE

Khalon and Zakiya's relationship was starting to pick up pace. They shopped for groceries together, jogged together, the two were inseparable. Day in and day out, they were together every chance they got. After working busy days, the two would lock themselves in Khalon's theater and watch movies until they fell asleep. They were always at Khalon's house.

Zakiya never bought Khalon to her place and it wasn't because his place could make ten of her apartments, but because she didn't want him to know where she stayed in case the two ever parted. If she didn't listen to anything else her mother Mary told her, she listened to her when she said, "Never bring the guys you meet in New York to the place where you lay your head. It's a crazy world and you just never know who to trust.

Bringing up a conversation out of nowhere, Zakiya told Khalon "I think you have the most beautiful house I have ever seen, Khalon. What would you do without me helping you bring life to it?"

Khalon rubbed Zakiya's arms with a soft touch up and down while she laid in his arms between his legs on his big, black sectional. "I don't know, but thank you for bringing life not only to my house, but to me. I think before you, I just existed. I wasn't really living. But now I have something to wake up to everyday. I don't dread going to work because I know if I don't, then my baby wont be able to get the Louboutin shoes she craves or the Gucci bags she yearns for."

Zakiya laid on Khalon's arms feeling safe. Life as she knew it was great. "You know you do not have to buy me Louboutin shoes and Gucci bags for me to love you, Khalon. Without it, I still hanker for your love. You like, give me comfort when I'm irritated, attention when I'm lonely. Hell, you are like my knight and armor guy. I desire your presence."

Khalon never had a woman talk to him like Zakiya. She was like a girl he had never met. Khalon had not felt this way about girl since his late wife. "You know if I wasn't buying the Gucci and Louboutin, the Chanel and Prada, you will be like this nigga cheap."

Zakiya laughed at Khalon's remark. "Yea, I'm not going to lie, I am a little high maintenance. I like nice things, so I'm not going to pretend like I don't. Do I look for the man to provide all the time? No. Do I think a man should provide most of the time? Yes. I like to be showered and wined but I can go without it, if my man is a good man. You know what I mean? Like I'm going to hustle for what I want regardless. But yeah, of course for a guy to have all of me, he has to have a career. He got to have time for me, and of course wine me every now and then because I will do the same, just not first."

Khalon laughed softly. "I feel you. There's nothing wrong with that. I really didn't care if you worked or not. As long as you keep me happy and on my feet, I will do my part and keep you happy. I know you're young, probably too young. That's why I have been avoiding asking you your age. You know daddy wants you happy, whatever it takes. I like your charm and personality so it's going to be a little hard to fall out of love with you."

Zakiya sat up from Khalon's chest and turned around, looking Khalon directly in the eye. Her look cut his statement short.

"Since when did you start loving me?" Zakiya asked with her lips tooting at the end of her sentence with her hazel eyes cutting sideways.

"I mean when I fall in love." The smirk on his face said it all, Khalon was embarrassed.

"Yeah, yeah, yeah," Zakiya said, laying back down.

"I was just kidding. What if I do love you? Would that scare you? I know it's only been five months, but what if I did love you?"

"Well, if you know that you did love me, I will tell you that I love you back."

Khalon kissed Zakiya on the top of her forehead and the two fell asleep in each other's arms.

αααα

Zakiya woke up in the morning vomiting all over Khalon's Persian rug. She couldn't hold the vomit. It came up full speed. She rushed to the bathroom trying to release what was left. Khalon couldn't help, but hear the loud coughing and vomiting in the restroom. When he stumbled off the sofa, he stepped right in Zakiya's throw up.

"Damn, what the hell is this? Baby, you alright in there?"

"Yea, I'm fine, baby. I'm sorry about your rug; I will get it cleaned or I will buy you another one if I have to," Zakiya said with vomit continuing to release out of her mouth.

Khalon washed his feet with a damp rag and did the same thing to his rug. He then took Zakiya some cold orange juice. "Here, baby drink this."

Zakiya took the orange juice and drank as much as she could. Within two seconds, she threw the juice right up.

"Baby, do you want to go to the hospital?"

Zakiya, kneeled in front of the toilet, nodded. "I thought I could take it, but I can't. My stomach is hurting too bad. If you don't mind, can you take me and stay with me too?"

"You don't have to ask me that, Kiya. Now, come on. Get up. I'm about to go get your clothes.

αααα

"I can't believe this. I feel like screaming at the top of my lungs right now. How could I miss this? I think I should go to another doctor and get a second opinion, Khalon. I just don't really believe that it's true. You know some tests can be wrong." Khalon was quiet in the Range Rover all the way back home from the doctor.

"I'm so sorry, but I didn't know, you got to believe me," Zakiya said to Khalon, looking at him while he drove. "Say something."

Khalon continued his silence.

Once they finally arrived at his house, he jumped out of the Rover, opening the door for Zakiya. The two walked in the house and sat at the dinner table. The silence surfaced the air for about five minutes before Khalon broke the silence. "I can never be mad at you. I care for you too much, but I do want you to be completely honest with me when you begin to tell me what's going on."

"Khalon when I first moved to New York, I met someone. We went out, until I found out that he was married. As soon as I found out, I told him that we couldn't date anymore. I never knew that the condom burst. I'm not expecting you to accept me and my condition Khalon. I will totally understand if you decide to leave me. There wouldn't be any bad blood between us because you heard what the doctor said-- I'm seven months. That's too far to have an abortion even if I wanted to, which I don't because I don't believe in them. I'm not sure what I am going to do. However, I know I can't, well, I don't want to tell the father. I want nothing to do with him. Besides, he is still married." Zakiya's tears rolled down her face in slow motion. She tried to catch them before they reached her chin. The last thing she wanted was for Khalon to feel sorry for her.

"Have you been listening to me at all Zakiya? I love you. I wouldn't abandon you for nothing. I couldn't stop loving you if I tried. I understand it's not your fault." Khalon lifted Zakiya out of her chair, and pulled her between his legs as he remained sitting in his chair. "I don't have kids and I will be more than happy to be the father to your baby girl if you will allow me. A new edition to the family will be great. This house of mine will surely be a home."

Zakiya was silent and Khalon was nervous. He didn't know if he was being too pushy, if he was moving too fast for Zakiya. All he was trying to do was express how he felt without freaking her out. "How about I give you some time to think about it and you just let me know? The last thing I want to do is to stress you or pressure you to do anything."

Zakiya bent down and kissed Khalon on the forehead. "You're not pressuring me to do anything. you couldn't, even if you wanted to. I like to think I'm too strong for that, but I will love for you to be the father to my baby girl. I think that's the best news I have heard all day." Khalon stood up with his broad shoulders and muscular arms, and wrapped them around Zakiya's body. He strolled his hands down to her round ass, since feeling Zakiya's round ass was the only thing he got to do. She told him that she didn't want to rush into having sex. That she wanted to learn more about him before taking it to that level. Khalon obeyed even though his lust for her was higher than the Empire State Building. Khalon tried lightening the mood in the room.

"Well, I guess we got some baby shopping to do."

"I guess we do. I guess I'm going to have to slow down on my shopping these days."

"Of course not. We are not hurting. Don't you worry about that. Your knight in armor is at your rescue."

Khalon's silly comment gave Zakiya the giggles. "Oh, I didn't know you were my hero."

"Yelp, I'm just out of uniform right now."

Khalon and Zakiya stood in the dining room, hugging each other while talking for about three minutes before they released the tight grip they had on one another. "How about you go lay down and I cook us up a good breakfast?"

"But we both have to go to work today, Khalon. I wasn't at the store yesterday and you didn't go into the restaurant or the station yesterday. We have to go today. Don't worry, I'm okay. In fact I'm great now that I know I got you on my side. I don't want to speed things up too fast. I want things to continue to flow like they have."

Khalon didn't agree. He thought they should speed things up just a little, but because he wanted to respect her and give her what she desired, he went along. "Okay Kiya, go easy today. You know what the doctor said."

"I am Khalon. I'm not even going to wear heels today. Muah. Zakiya kissed Khalon on his lips.

αααα

"Hey honey, I haven't seen you in a minute," Saran greeted Zakiya with a huge smile.

"I know, we never seem to work on the same day any more."

"Don't you look normal and comfortable today?" Zakiya wore her inexpensive yet comfortable black and white Dotted Line leggings and a comfortable black cotton V-neck shirt and she finished off her outfit with a Burberry Haymarket Check bag.

"Oh well thank you, that's the look I was going for. How is everything going here?"

"Oh, things are fine but I do have something to tell you as usual. So when you get time, come to the register and holler at me."

"Well, I got time now." Zakiya walked behind the register, standing beside Saran.

Saran reached in her purse and grabbed her phone out, handing it to Zakiya. "Read that text from your neighbor."

Zakiya took the phone and read the text. "Tell your friend her secret is no longer a secret." Zakiya's heart dropped to her knees. Her palms began sweating like they do when her nerves start to scatter. "What the hell is she talking about?"

"Girl, I don't know. That's why I just gave the phone to you. I'm through with trying to figure it out. That girl is starting to get on my last nerves. Oh yeah, I meant to tell you, Jarlath's wife came by to see you."

Zakiya turned to Saran with her eyes wide. "Alayne came by looking for me? For what? When? How could you forget to tell me that?"

"Slow down. I forgot to tell you but I called you like three times when she came in. You just never answered your phone. She said she left a message on your phone. I figured you got it and just weren't interested."

Zakiya remembered when Saran called, but she had ignored it because she and Khalon were sleeping and she didn't want to wake him up with the talking.

"She said it was important and that she needed to talk to you. Just check your answering machine and see for yourself."

Zakiya sat down in the chair behind the register. "I'm not about to bust my head wide open trying to figure out what that damn lady wanted. Anyways, have you eaten? I'm hungry and about to order me some wings."

"Nawl, I haven't. You know I'm down."

αααα

It was time to close the store and Zakiya was tired. She told Khalon that she wasn't coming by his house tonight. She needed some time alone. There was just too much going on in one day and she needed some quality time to suck it all up. Zakiya thought that Khalon would put up a fight but he didn't. He accepted her not coming to his house very easily. Zakiya locked all the doors and windows in the store, and cut the lights off before she went to her apartment.

BOOM, BOOM, KNOCK, BOOM, KNOCK! The heavy knocks on the door startled Zakiya. She looked out the window with her heart beating faster than ever. Five tall built guys dressed in long black coats and gloves stood outside. Zakiya didn't know what to do. She ran upstairs to her apartment. Heart racing and palms sweaty, Zakiya kept her eyes wide open, checking the scene in every room before entering. It's September and the weather isn't cold enough for long coats and gloves. Zakiya thought to herself.

After ten long minutes of pounding on the doors and back windows, the men left. "Maybe they had the wrong building."

To calm her nerves Zakiya decided to check her messages, so she could see what it was that Alayne wanted with her. When she called her voicemail, the message was already checked.

"Dang, I must have called my voicemail again. I need to set up my password that way it won't go directly to my messages."

"Press four to hear your old messages." The operator demanded professionally.

Zakiya dialed two to listen to Alayne's message over accepting the fact that she called her voicemail by mistake again.

"Hello, this is Alayne. You need to call me as soon as possible. Your life is in danger!

Jarlath knows about you being pregnant. I can't tell you too much over the phone so meet me at Jacob's bar Wednesday at 8:30 and come alone. Make sure that you are not being trailed."

"To delete this message, please press three. To save this message, please press four."

Zakiya dialed four. She didn't know what to think. She didn't know how to feel. She packed her things as fast as she could. She decided to go to Khalon's house until she figured out what was going on.

On her way down the stairs she heard a loud "BOOM!" She stopped in the hallway listening hard for strange noise. Zakiya walked down the stairs slowly lips quivering and eyes wet, she fought hard, trying to hold back the tears that were demanded to flow. She didn't know who was in the store but she was certain they were in.

"Shush. Be quiet and stop knocking over shit," one of the intruders said echoing from the store kitchen. Zakiya remained silent. If they were robbers, then she was going to let them take whatever they wanted. Her life was more important. Zakiya tried to walk back up to the apartment, but they could hear her footsteps in the hallway.

"Zakiya, is that you?"

Zakiya released a deep breath. The voice was a girl's.

"Who is there?"

"This Cambria, girl. Come open the door!"

Zakiya forgot all about Cambria coming to town. She eventually called Cambria when she felt better. The morning sickness had her stuck. Cambria was extra excited to come see her since they weren't that far away.

"Hey, baby sister. Oh, and that spare key wasn't where you said it was. It took me five minutes to find that key."

Zakiya stood in the store looking at her sister who couldn't have come at a worst time. Zakiya didn't want to scare nor bother Cambria with her dangerous dilemmas so she placed a smile on her face even though she wasn't happy at all. "I'm happy to see you. Hey Harley, yawl come on. Grab your things and come on upstairs."

Harley and Cambria followed Zakiya upstairs. "I would have never known this was an apartment. It's so secretive."

"I know that's how I like it. Now did yall lock the door back behind you?"

"Yea, we did."

SISTERLY LOVE

Cambria stood in the seating area with her hands on her hips, catching her breath from the stairs. For about sixty seconds Cambria stood in the living room, taking a good look at the apartment.

"I can't believe my little sister is all grown up and on her own."

Zakiya gave a fake giggle. She tried her best to stay focused and not lead her sister to suspicions.

"Your apartment is nice, little sister. I mean damn, this furniture is real nice. Hell, it's bigger than the apartment Harley and me got." Cambria walked around the house, admiring Zakiya's nice things. "This furniture looks expensive as shit."

Harley nodded his head, sitting down on the sofa. "The store must be doing real good, Zakiya?"

Zakiya continued to put away Cambria's things in the hallway closet. "Yall don't mind sleeping in the living room, do you?"

"No, that's no problem. As nice as this apartment is, I'm going to enjoy laying in here. Cambria dug her shoes into the carpet.

Don't worry about Harley because he is leaving." Cambria added throwing her hand up at Harley.

"Oh, he is? Why?"

"He is going to meet his cousin out in Harlem."

"Oh, okay. I forgot he did say he had family in New York."

"Yea, I am going to let you girls catch up. You are doing damn good too, Zakiya. Shoot, my cousins have lived in New York all their life and haven't gotten to the point where you at. I mean, Manhattan is like very expensive. How the heck are you surviving here?"

Zakiya sat down finally on the sofa next to Cambria. "Well, the store is doing great so that helps me out a lot."

"Oh, okay, well I'm going to let you girls catch up. Cambria, I will call you when I get there."

"Okay Harley."

On the way to Zakiya's room Cambria noticed the beautiful paintings on the wall. "Zakiya you collect paintings now?" Zakiya who was in front of Cambria turned back and responded, "not really, I just seen them paintings and I really like them so I bought them, but I would like to start my own collection." As soon as the girls entered the bedroom Cambria bomb rushed Zakiya's closet.

"Look at all these clothes and shoes you got girl, expensive stuff too," Cambria said, strolling through Zakiya's top name dresses and looking at her high priced pumps. "Oh you are living big time, Miss Thing. Every shoe in this closet got a comma on the price tag and you got dresses you haven't even worn yet."

"All those shoes do not have commas on the price tag. I like all kinds of shoes. What can I say? I'm a shoe freak. Plus when you work hard you have to treat yourself." Zakiya sat on the bed watching Cambria try on things in her closet.

"Doesn't it feel so good to be out of Georgia? Cambria face was lit with joy. You know grown and on your own?"

Zakiya smiled and this time it was a real one. "Yea, it does. You know I thank God every day for my blessings. I've been doing everything I said I wanted to do. I just sent my synopsis to Simon and Schuster so I'm waiting on a response from them. My store is doing great and I'm able to financially support whatever craving I have."

Cambria sat on the bed next to Zakiya. "This is a big bed for one person and it's comfortable. Anyways, I see that you are doing great. I mean, I can barely believe you are turning to one of those power success women that you read about in books or see on TV, very career oriented. But how is your personal life?" Cambria asked out of curiosity.

Zakiya smiled. "At first I was like enjoying the single life, you know? I'm young, beautiful, and successful. So I wasn't in a big rush to be locked down."

"So, why are you talking in past tense then?"

"Just listen, let me tell this story."

"Okay, okay."

"I have had some of the most wonderful dates a girl could ever ask for. I'm talking very expensive ones too, Cambria. Then out of nowhere, I meet this wonderful, sexy, single, career oriented guy."

Cambria's mouth was watering.

"And we've been inseparable since."

"Ah come on Zakiya, for an author, you sure is low on details."

Zakiya burst out laughing. She knew Cambria was edging for more. "What, he is an amazing guy, very successful. He is like one of New York's greatest detectives and he owns a very successful restaurant and club. So the money is good."

"I think New York has shaped you up, I mean, you know changed you. You are so not the little Zakiya from Jackson anymore. Oh yea, speaking of Jackson. Guess who got kicked out of school and is back in Jackson?"

"Who, girl!" Zakiya asked with big eyes.

"Your boy, Bailey." Cambria shook her head.

"Um, see, God don't like ugly." Zakiya pointed her index finger to Cambria shaking her head side-to-side with Cambria.

"Momma says he has been asking about you non-stop. Talking about can he have your number? Momma said, "she in New York living the good life, she's not trying to talk to you.""

"Momma said that Cambria?" Zakiya stared at Cambria for about ten seconds with her eyes bigger. She was shocked to hear that her mother was bragging on her living in New York.

"Yea, honey, I was on the phone when she said it."

"Momma got a little buck in the system." The girls laughed about two minutes at Zakiya's joke.

"I guess I should tell you."

Cambria eyes broadened. "I knew it was something juicy you had to tell me. Spill it trick." Cambria responded to Zakiya with excitement.

"Okay, I will just come right out and say it. I'm pregnant." Cambria's mouth was wide open. "You are lying little girl. Are you serious?"

"Yes, I am."

"How far are you, like three weeks or something?"

"Try seven months."

Cambria stood up off the bed and took Zakiya's hands and stood her on her feet. "Where are you seven months at Zakiya?"

"I said the same thing but I had my ultrasound and everything. I'm having a baby girl."

"But you are so small."

"I know, I wouldn't even know I was pregnant if I didn't go to the hospital because I had no symptom's. I still can't believe it, but I am. I am due on November the 12th."

"Wow, I'm going to be an aunt. We got to call Momma and the rest of them to tell them Zakiya. You know I can't keep a secret that big away from them."

"I wasn't expecting you to with your big mouth." The girls were good and sleepy after staying up with their screaming sisters and over protective momma. Mary didn't know how to respond. One minute she was praying for Zakiya, asking God to please forgive her for her sin and the next minute she was coming up with baby names.

αααα

"You weren't lying when you said your store is doing great. It's been packed all day."

"Yea, I know. When Saran comes in, we can go out somewhere and have brunch or something."

"I swear your stomach looks bigger today than it did last night." Cambria rubbed Zakiya stomach in a circular motion.

"Hey Saran, I was just talking about you." Zakiya didn't give Saran time to approach the register before she spoke. "Meet my sister, Cambria. Cambria, this is Saran, a close friend."

You could see all of Saran teeth's as she waved at Cambria, she was glad to be introduced as a close friend. "Hey, how are you?"

"I'm fine. You got a lot on your plate today. It's been busy all morning," Cambria said to Saran.

"I know, it usually is, but the busier the better. More money, plus it makes time go by much faster."

"Well Saran I'm leaving. I'm going to take Cambria out for brunch. I will be back. Okay?"

"Sure, have fun."

"We will."

THE MEETING

The weekend went by like a track star-- fast. Cambria and Harley left and Zakiya was already missing them even though she wasn't up for them staying when they first came. After they left, she decided to just have herself some time away from work and friends. Zakiya and Khalon hadn't seen each other since the day she found out she was having a baby girl. He couldn't take it no more, so Khalon surprised her with beautiful fruit flowers and a Gucci baby bag.

"Khalon, you didn't have to buy me anything. However, I do like the Gucci baby bag."

"I missed you little lady. Why haven't you been by the house this weekend? I tried to give you your space, but I see you will never come around if I don't." Khalon stood at the register with the fruit flowers in his hands.

"Don't be like that Khalon. You know that's not true." Zakiya walked away from the register. "Kelly, come grab the register for me sweetheart," Zakiya said to one of the new workers. She then led Khalon to the back where the tables were. "I told you my sister and her fiancé were here this weekend, so I had to entertain them. That's the only reason why I didn't come by. In fact I was on my way out to your house when they came."

Khalon pulled out the chair for Zakiya. "So, why you didn't introduce me to your family? I would have loved to meet them."

"And you will sooner than later." Zakiya responded quickly. "Oh, I'm closing the store early today. I have something I need to do. What time is it?" Zakiya looked at her phone to check the time.

"7:30," Khalon responded. "You are going to close the store down early on a Wednesday?"

"Yeah, I got to do something. I will be by the house tonight though, so prepare me something delicious to eat." Khalon didn't ask what Zakiya had to do, he was just happy to know that she was coming by the house tonight. He kissed Zakiya on the lips gently before leaving, "I'll see you tonight baby, call me when you're on the way." "Okay, I will." Zakiya responded, she looked at her phone again, checking the time. She took two grapes from the fruit basket, shoved them in her mouth and zoomed out the store leaving Kelly the keys to lock up. Zakiya was eager to see what Alayne had to say, so she didn't want to waste any time. After arriving at the location, she scoped out her surroundings and for the first time in three days she wasn't being followed. The Jacob bar was packed which made it very difficult to find Alayne. Instead of walking around looking mysterious, Zakiya decided to sit at the bar so Alayne could scope her out. And like clockwork, there was Alayne.

"Hey, follow me outside," Alayne whispered to Zakiya.

Once they got outside, Alayne checked out the surroundings. Then Alayne jumped right into it. "Jarlath is planning to kill you. He knows you are pregnant and he feels like you betrayed him. He will jump through fire to have kids and the fact that you haven't told him angers him."

"So why are you telling me this? Isn't he your husband? Aren't you even mad at all about him cheating on you? And why are you whispering?"

Alayne grabbed Zakiya's arms and walked her slowly towards the trash cans in the back alley. "Because I could be jeopardizing my life as well, Miss Thing, trying to save your ass. You don't know who you're dealing with. Jarlath is a very powerful man and playing with him is like suicide. Yes, I know you two where messing around. Jarlath and I been over with. What, you thought I didn't hear you at the fashion show. I just ignored you sweetie because I didn't care."

"So why hasn't he killed me yet? His bodyguards have been following me for the last few days."

"He is not going to kill you until you have your baby. The plan is to kidnap you and have his private doctor deliver the baby. Jarlath will do anything for a family and if you think you are going to have a baby and not include him, you are wrong."

Zakiya's heart was pounding. She knew what Alayne was saying had to have truth in it. "Oh, and that little bright light detective you have been dating is not exactly safe either. That friend Makeeda of yours is the person who told Jarlath you were pregnant. She had seen you at the doctor and told Jarlath. That's when Jarlath threatened the doctor for information."

Zakiya with tears in her eyes stood speechless. She didn't understand how her life that was once great, slowly was turning into a disaster. "So what do you suggest I do?"

Alayne straightened her back, looking around with water in her eyes. "Look, I only wanted to warn you. What you do with the information is your business." Alayne felt sorry for the young girl, but there was nothing she could do even if she wanted to help. She was hanging on by a thread herself. "Just know this, there is nothing that goes on in New York that Jarlath don't know about. So your best bet is to be honest with him or leave New York because it's really too late for apologies now. He's really not a forgiving man. I have to go. Just be careful and take care of yourself." Alayne walked off at full speed, looking like a nervous wreck, checking her surroundings.

Zakiya walked off right after her, the exact same way, watching her back. Right after leaving the bar Zakiya went straight to Khalon's house. With what all that was going on, she needed to be held. She needed to feel protected. On the way to Khalon's house Zakiya thoughts were racing, so she knew the entire time that we were messing around, man what have I gotten myself into. Let me not think about this tonight. Lord I ask if you will please keep me safe. Finally, Zakiya arrived at Khalon's house; before entering she took a deep breath and fixed her hair, when she opened the door Khalon jumped up off the sofa as if he was about to attack her.

"It's me, it's me, I didn't mean to scare you."

"It's okay, baby, come on in. I just forgot that you were coming. Come on in, I fixed your favorite. Hot Wings and house fried rice." Zakiya was happy to hear Khalon say the words hot wings. Hot wings always made Zakiya feel good.

"You look so tense baby, how has things been at the station?"

Khalon walked to the kitchen and heated up Zakiya's food for her. From the kitchen he answered, "Not too good. I'm still working on this Kilo case. I promised his mother I would find the killer but the man who I know is responsible is hard to nail."

Zakiya walked in the kitchen so that she could give Khalon some support. She knew he had a long day and she wanted to be an ear for him to talk to since she was always using his ear. Zakiya had seen that Khalon only fixed one plate. "You not going to eat baby?"

"Naw, I ate earlier. I need to finish some things on this case anyway."

"So who do you think is responsible Khalon?"

"Well, I'm sure this man Jarlath is behind it but I can't get the evidence I need to stick. He is very powerful and weak evidence is something his very expensive lawyers will eat up in court."

Zakiya's heart began racing for the second time in one day. "How powerful?" Zakiya asked curiously.

"Have you ever heard of the Illuminati?"

"Yea, I have. I'm not too sure about it in detail but I have heard a little something about it."

"Well, he's that powerful. He is the president. So it's almost impossible to catch him doing anything." Zakiya read some of the magazines and newspaper articles about Kilo's death. There are speculations that rapper Kilo was killed for speaking against the Illuminati. Rapper Kilo set up by mentor, grammy award winning rapper Kilo shot down in Central Park.

"And you think he is responsible for the rapper Kilo's death?" Zakiya asked looking Khalon directly in the eyes.

Khalon sat at the bar with Zakiya while she ate. "I know he's responsible."

Zakiya begin to eat her food, thinking about how she was going to handle her situation. "I read about that Kilo's incident in the papers. It was sad. I really liked him. He was what we call in Georgia an educated rapper. Meaning he didn't just rap about anything. His lyrics had meaning."

"Yeah, he was great. We grew up in the same neighborhood. I saw him grow from a young boy to a grown man. That's why it's important for me to catch his killer. I always had an obsession with the Illuminati."

"I can see why. You are a good man and I'm sure you want justice brought for the innocent's sake."

"Yeah, that's why I need to go to work on some things, so if you don't mind beautiful, I will excuse myself."

"Okay sexy, you are excused." Zakiya leaned her head down. She had more problems piling up on more problems. Now Khalon, her new love, was working on her secret baby daddy's case, trying to put him away for murder. Zakiya couldn't wrap her fingers around all of her problems in one night. There was just too much going on. Her mind felt like exploding. Then she remembered something her mother always told her, "When things get too heavy for you to handle, just let go and let God deal with it." Zakiya decided to take her mother's advice. Besides, it was the only option. There was nothing she could do about her complicated life at the moment. Zakiya took her food and placed the rest in the microwave.

"Baby, I'm going to go upstairs. I'm getting a little tired, plus the baby is starting to get irritated."

Khalon walked towards Zakiya who was heading up the stairs and gave her the longest tongue kiss in the history of kissing. "I love you. I will be up soon to hold you."

"Okay, I'm going to take a long bubble bath so you have time to do your little research or whatever you sexy detectives do these days." Zakiya kissed Khalon on the lips and continued up the stairs. Tired, Zakiya was ready to take a hot bath and call it a night.

Before diving into her relaxing bubble bath, she kneeled down to say a prayer. "Heavenly father, I come to you as humble as I know how. I confess my sins, those known and unknown. Lord, you know I'm not perfect and I fall short every day of my life. I just want to take time out to say thank you. Thank you for your mercy. I have more bills than money, but thank you for my home, car, food, and life, everything I do have. I realize that this life I'm living is full of trial and tribulations but thank you for not putting more on me than I can bear. In your Holy name I pray AMEN."

Zakiya stood up on her feet stretching and yawning. Then she dived into her warm bubble bath that was waiting patiently for her. She felt better about her life already. Zakiya had to remember that she was a Christian going girl and that there wasn't anything the good Lord couldn't handle. It was so many people claiming to be powerful in New York that Zakiya almost forgot that God was the only man with great power.

THE WHOLE TRUTH

Zakiya woke up to the sweet smell of bacon, cheese eggs, and cheese grits, her favorite. Khalon brought Zakiya breakfast in bed.

"Aw, baby you cooked me breakfast? You shouldn't have!" Zakiya laughed at her smart comment.

"I know madam. I'm at your service. Anything else you need?"

"Yes, one hot long kiss."

Khalon cut Zakiya's laughing off with her request. He gave her one long, passionate tongue kiss. "Eat up, I got the day planned out for us. C clear your schedule and that's not an option, young lady. The day belongs to you and me."

"I got you, captain, I got you." Zakiya called Saran in to manage the store. Not that she had to-- she had promoted Saran to manager and she was doing great with the position.

ααααα

"Baby, where are we going?"

Khalon took Zakiya by the hand and ignored her question. Together they walked into one of New York's most expensive baby stores.

"Hello, welcome to Luxury Babies," the thin Caucasian blonde retailer said. "Is there anything I can help you with?"

"Yes, as a matter fact, you can. We are here to buy the most beautiful crib you have in the store."

"Sure, that's no problem, and do we know the sex?"

"Yes, a baby girl," Zakiya responded. "Aw, baby look at these adorable booties. OMG! I think I'm going to hurt the wallet in this store. I want this," Zakiya said pointing to a Gucci stroller and car seat set. "I also want this lovely Gucci pacifier. I'll take that lovely swing set as well."

Khalon watched as Zakiya shopped for their unborn. Smiling, it was the first time all day, that the two was at ease. They weren't thinking about the problems that were circulating around their life. Zakiya looked at the crib one last time before deciding it was the one.

"Baby, are sure you know how to put up that crib before we leave?"

Khalon quickly responded, "Yes, baby, I got you."

"Khalon, I'm not playing with you."

"I know how to put up the crib. It's nothing I can't do, girl. You haven't learned that yet."

"Oh right, I hear you."

"In fact you can give me that purple and pink paint. We need to do some painting as well."

Zakiya did her signature eye brow raise. "And who is going to paint Khalon?"

"We are my love."

αααα

"You are getting that paint everywhere, Khalon."

Khalon charged toward Zakiya with the paint brush as if he was going to paint her face.

"Quit playing! Damn, you are going to end up getting that shit in my hair."

Khalon stopped in his tracks with the brush in his hands, confused. He had never heard Zakiya speak that way. His heart sunk in like quick sand, he realized it wasn't impossible for a man's feelings to get hurt. He tried hard to let his anger catch up with his patience before speaking. Khalon paused for about five minutes before asking Zakiya, "Are you straight and I'm hoping not because if you are, that tone and me don't match. I mean at all."

Zakiya stood still and broke down, pressing her hands to her face and crying as hard as she could. "I'm sorry Khalon. I'm so sorry. You haven't been anything less than great to me. I just have so much on my mind right now."

Khalon wrapped his hands around Zakiya's body. "Baby calm down, don't get yourself upset like this."

Zakiya gathered her tears and sat down on the floor in the empty baby room. "I have something to tell you, Khalon. I just can't hold it in any longer."

Khalon looked like he lost his heart already. He didn't know what to think. He sat next to Zakiya on the floor. "What is it Zakiya? And skip the long path. Give it to me straight up." Khalon said with his baritone voice, without a teeth or dimple in sight.

"I never told you who the father of my baby was."

Khalon took a deep breath and said, "So, continue."

"So, he is Jarlath."

Khalon jumped up on his feet and punched a huge hole in the wall. Zakiya broke down crying once more. "I'm sorry, Khalon. I wanted to tell you, I just

174

didn't know how to tell you, baby. Please don't be mad at me. The last thing I need is for you to be mad at me, Khalon."

Khalon leaned his head against the unpainted wall it and tried his best to fight back the tears that were beginning to form. Zakiya walked up behind him, rubbing his broad shoulders, kissing his back. "If you want me to leave, I understand, Khalon. I do. You have been too good to me for me to ignore your request. So just say the word and I will leave."

After five minutes of silence, Khalon turned to face the lady that witnessed him shed a tear. "Do you want to leave, Zakiya?" Khalon asked with wrinkles on his fore head.

"Khalon, I don't want to leave but I don't want to be a burden either."

Khalon wiped his face dry and hugged Zakiya tight. "I love you more than a little bit, so I'm going to fight for what I know we are destined for. I just ask that you please don't keep anything else from me."

Zakiya pushed away from Khalon and said, "There is more."

Khalon looked at Zakiya and said "Spill Zakiya, stop holding back on me."

"Jarlath wants me dead because I haven't told him about the baby. His boys have been following me for some time now and I think they are following you too. At least that's what his wife told me."

"Oh, you don't have to worry about that I dare him to try anything crazy. Trust me it will make my year, from now on though you are to come here every night. After work, you come straight here until I can get this resolved."

Zakiya's silence made Khalon ask her, "Are you willing to work with me on this Zakiya?"

"Yes, Khalon I hear you baby. I'm not going to keep anything from you and I promise I will come straight home after work. It's probably best right now anyway with the baby on the way and all."

Khalon hugged Zakiya again and for another five minutes, the room was silent, the two just enjoying each other's company. "Let's finish this tomorrow. I just want to go lie down and hold you in my arms until the sun wakes back up." Zakiya agreed. The two walked out of the baby's room and quickly into the master bedroom, holding each other while kissing each other's face off.

THE BIG ARRIVAL

Zakiya paced the floor all night. The contractions were about an hour apart, and finally, her water broke. "Khalon wake up! It's time, my water just broke!" Zakiya said, shaking Khalon in his sleep.

"What is it? What is it?" Khalon said, turning the opposite way from Zakiya.

"WAKE UP KHALON, MY WATER JUST BROKE!"

Khalon, half-asleep, jumped to his feet and ran to the closet, grabbing the baby bag they packed together. "Are you dressed, Zakiya?" Khalon was running around like a kid at the playground with no direction.

"Khalon what are you doing? You don't even have clothes on. Where are you going?" Khalon only had on his Hanes socks and his polo briefs, running out the master room with the Gucci baby bag on his shoulders. "Baby you got to put on some clothes."

"Oh yeah, that's right." Khalon dropped the bag and ran to the closet to get dressed. Zakiya was already dressed. She knew that her baby girl was coming earlier than expected so she called the doctor the moment the contractions became consistent. "Are you ready Khalon?"

"Yea momma I'm coming, I'm putting on my shoes." Khalon took Zakiya hand and walked her down the stairs and off to Mercy General Hospital they went.

αααα

"Zakiya, your baby girl will be here sooner than you think. Are you ready to be a mother?"

Zakiya smiled at the short, Chinese doctor. "Yes, I'm ready. I will be a mother soon and the anxiety is killing me."

Khalon laughed hard. "Oh don't worry, you are about to enter a point of no return very soon. There will never be just a Zakiya ever again. You will be, 'Hey, I'm Zakiya and this is my baby girl.'"

Zakiya thought Khalon made a great point. She was living the last moments of her single life. Soon she was about to be responsible for another human's life. Just the thought of it gave Zakiya the chills. "I think I have to use the restroom, Dr. Hung."

Dr. Hung turned around from the charts he was reading. "What number are you talking, Ms. Kiya?"

"The number where more than liquid comes out." Khalon thought Zakiya's choice of words was brilliant. "Nice, now how are you going to do that?" Khalon asked looking at Zakiya with his eyes wide and left eye brow raised. The doctor pulled back the white sheet and took a look between Zakiya legs.

"It's time for your baby girl Zakiya. I want you to open your legs for me, sweetie."

"But I don't feel anything, at least nothing like the girls off the TV. I guess the drugs are working." Zakiya practically pulled her baby out on her own.

178

"It's a baby girl, Zakiya, congratulations!" Dr. Hung said.

Khalon cut the umbilical cord. "She is beautiful, come on open them eyes let me see you, come on beautiful." Khalon watched the nurses wrap the baby up. "There you go princess," Khalon said walking the baby to Zakiya. "She opened her eyes, my goodness her eyes are beautiful and big too." Khalon just watched as Zakiya kissed her on the forehead. You should name her Niara meaning large eyes," the doctor requested.

"That's it! I'm going to name her Naira. Naira Lee."

"That's beautiful, I love that." Khalon skipped asking Zakiya to give Naira his last name. He didn't want to ask her if she didn't ask him first. He decided to just enjoy the moment. "I'm ready to go home now." Khalon said looking at his family.

"Wow! For the first time in a long time, I'm ready to go home. Khalon nodded his head as he repeated his comment, checking himself. We are parents now, Zakiya."

"I know, right? It's going to be a long, interesting, but a fun ride baby. Are you ready?"

"More than you know."

WORD OF ADVICE

Khalon finally went back to work after staying home for two weeks helping Zakiya out with the baby. Saran took over the store while Zakiya remained on maternity leave.

"Baby, have a nice day," Zakiya said, kissing Khalon on the cheeks before he walked out the door.

"I will try, but I'm not holding my breath. Try not to be on your feet too long and call me if you need anything."

"I will, Khalon. Try not to worry too much. Naira and me will be fine."

Khalon kissed Zakiya on her lips and walked out the door. Zakiya was relieved that Khalon was gone. Now she could finally call her mother, like she has wanted to do for some time now. Naira was asleep in her crib so Zakiya took her phone and the baby monitor with her to the living room. After the second ring, Mary picked up the phone.

"Hey Momma, how are you?"

Mary smiled. She not only got to hear her daughter's voice, but her voice with joy in it as well. "Well I'm fine and you?"

"Oh I'm great."

"Where is my grandbaby?"

"She's asleep finally. That girl does not sleep like most infants, I'm telling you. I sometimes have to pray for her to go to sleep."

Mary laughed at her daughter who was now a mother. "Welcome to motherhood. You know you have to wrap her up tight in a blanket. That way she will feel like she is still in the wound and she will sleep way longer."

"Oh for real, Momma?"

"Yeah, Zakiya. When are you going to bring my granddaughter to see me?"

Zakiya froze. "I don't know Momma, hopefully soon. I don't know if I want to put her on the plane just yet."

"I know you better bring my grandchild to see me. And where is this amazing guy I keep hearing about?"

"Oh, he went back to work today. He took a two week sick leave to be with Naira and me. Did you get the pictures I sent you?"

"Yes I did and they were beautiful. I just can't wait to hold my granddaughter. The first of many to come."

"Cambria is supposed to be coming to see her, but where is Grandma? Momma, isn't she there with you?"

"Yeah, as a matter of fact she is. Did you want to speak with her?"

"Yeah, if you don't mind."

"Don't see why I would, hold on. She is in the living room. Let me get her for you."

Zakiya was anxious to speak to her grandma. Annabella was the only person Zakiya knew that had knowledge on the Illuminati and she wasn't so uptight like her mother so she wouldn't freak out if Zakiya asked her questions concerning it.

"Hey, baby."

"Hey Grandma, how are you doing?"

"I'm great now that I hear one of my granddaughter's voice. How has the New York life been treating you?"

"Oh well you know, full of surprises. It's been keeping me on my feet so far."

"It wouldn't be New York if it didn't."

"Grandma, I have a question to ask you, if you don't mind?"

Annabella and Mary knew when Zakiya said, "If you don't mind," she was trying to sweeten them up for the news to come. "No, I don't Zakiya. What do you have to ask me?"

"Well I have a friend that has a situation. She kind of, you know, met this guy. They went out, had like this amazing time. She kind of like got to his heart like no other lady has been able to. Now this guy is very powerful."

"What do you mean by powerful Zakiya? I need details if I'm going to give accurate advice."

"Like Illuminati powerful." Annabella ears were more alert than ever.

"Anyways, to make a long story short, she kind of broke up with him when she found out that he was married even though he assured her that he was in the divorce stage and that they were legally separated. Then my friend got pregnant by this guy because the condom broke. You know she did practice safe sex."

"Right, that Christian girl wouldn't do something like not practicing safe sex. I know, she's just not that kind of girl," Annabella said, being sarcastic.

Zakiya didn't catch on. Instead, she continued babbling. "She never told him about the baby and when he found out, it kind of wrinkled his forehead a little. Now she hears that he has a hit out for her. So I guess what I'm asking is, how much do you know about the Illuminati?"

"Do you know if this guy is the head of the Illuminati or is he just a member?"

"I'm pretty sure she said he was the leader."

"Well, most likely if he is the leader and cared for you, Zakiya, him killing you will be the last on the list. Men in that position value their families. Is Naira his first child?"

Zakiya's heart dropped to her stomach. She didn't understand how her grandma assumed she was talking about herself, especially when she was being extra careful not to lead her to that conclusion. But she was tired of lying. "Yes, Naira is his only child but Khalon has agreed to raise Naira as his own."

"That will be your first mistake. I know you think this Khalon guy is great, but if he is not Naira's father and Naira's father is willing to be her father, then by the Bible and by law he should."

"Hold on Grandma, are you around Momma?"

"No child, she is in her room. Nine time out of ten, this powerful guy only wants to get your attention. He only wants to talk to you. Now, do I believe that your love Khalon's life is in danger? Yes. Because a man with power likes his prize possessions to himself especially if it's his family. You need to go and talk to Naira's father, baby, because if you don't then and only then will things get dangerous. Don't test his love for you because sometimes men like to think if they can't have her no one will and that's not the state we want this guy to enter. Do you hear me?"

"Yes, Grandma and I thank you for your advice. I really needed it."

"Now this secret only stays a secret for a minute. So I'm going to need you to get on the move. As soon as you talk to this guy, call me and if you don't do it soon, I am telling your mother. And you know how that's going to go."

"Yes I do. Don't worry I'm going to do just that. In fact before calling you, I had that on the option table."

"Okay, Zakiya, I trust you to be responsible."

"I got you, Grandma. Thank you." As soon as Zakiya hung up the phone with her grandma, someone was knocking at the door.

"Hold on, I'm coming." Zakiya looked out the peep hole and it was Saran.

"Come in. Is everything alright at the store?" Zakiya asked Saran before she could even get in the door.

"Yeah, everything is all right. I just wanted to let you know that these guys dressed in all black came by the store. They had guns on their sides and everything, Zakiya, and they were looking for you. I knew this has to do something with that damn Jarlath. So I had to run and tell you. The guy told me to tell you that Jarlath is looking for you and for you to get in touch with him as soon as possible, for your safety." Saran was shaking, pacing the floor with both of her hands pressed together making a big fist. "I just wish he will leave you alone already. Where is Khalon? We should tell him so he can protect you." Saran was losing her mind. It was like her own life was in danger.

Zakiya watched calmly, looking at her friend who was a nervous wreck. She never told Saran about Jarlath searching for her, Saran just knew that he was going through fire to try and make her jealous, by messing with Makeeda, Zakiya didn't want to scare her so she didn't include her on all the drama in her life. Saran didn't even know that Zakiya was pregnant until she had the baby. "Don't stress yourself Saran. I'm glad you came by to tell me."

"Why are you so calm, Zakiya? You know what this man is capable of! He is not the man to play with."

"I know Saran. I'm going to handle it. You just calm down."

The loud two voices woke Naira who was sleeping in the room upstairs. She began crying letting her mother know she was awake. "I'm sorry, did I wake the baby up? Awl I am sorry."

"Don't worry about it. It's about time for her to wake up anyway. Do you want to hold her?"

"Yeah, you know I will."

Zakiya ran upstairs to get the beautiful crying Naira. "Here she is," Zakiya said, placing Naira in Saran's hands.

"Oh, she is so beautiful. Look at all this hair she got, Zakiya. I can't believe you are a mother now. When I first met you, you were a little snobby, single chick. Now look at you. You have everything a girl could ask for, besides the murder hunt thing."

Zakiya and Saran both laughed at the joke. Saran's eyes suddenly widened. "You little trick, I get it now. Jarlath is Naira's father, isn't he?"

Zakiya sat down on the sofa. "Don't you keep me in the dark, Zakiya! Is he the father?"

"Yes Saran, he is the father."

"OMG! He's going to try and hurt my God baby. We got to tell someone." Saran began to freak out again, holding Naira close to her chest.

"Calm down, Saran. He is not going to hurt Naira. I told you I got a plan."

"Do you need me to do anything?"

"If I do, I will tell you. Until then, I just need you to stay grounded and don't tell anyone anything."

"Okay, you know I'm not, that's your business I wouldn't do that." Saran placed Naira in

Zakiya's arms carefully." "Well, I got to go. My lunch break is almost up. I need to get back to the store. Call me if you need me for anything."

"I promise you, I will." Saran walked out the door and Zakiya sat on the sofa taking her breast out, feeding Naira and feeling good about her plan.

"Here Mommy's baby."

HIM OR ME

"Come in and shut the door behind you."

"Jarlath, we got a problem. We found out who killed Kilo. You wouldn't believe who either."

Jarlath looked Quake Man in the eyes, daring him to try his suspicion. "I know who killed Kilo as well but I'm interested to see who you think did it, so spill."

"Ronny, that nigga you grew up with back in the day. That nigga wanted to get in the Illuminati since he heard about it. My source tells me that his plan is to set you up. He's trying to make it look like you did it."

"Wow! You are a genius. Now how long did it take you to figure that out?"

Quake Man sat down in the expensive leather seat that Jarlath had sitting in front of his desk. The mug on Jarlath's face told Quake Man the boss wasn't too pleased with the news. So Quake Man knew there was more. "So you already knew all this I see," Quake said to Jarlath thinking, damn I'm late.

"Yeah, you see my source works a little bit faster than yours."

"Well, did your source tell you that your precious wife may be involved as well?"

Jarlath's eyes wandered away from Quake Man, watching Manhattan out his tall windows. He placed his hands on his chin, showing no emotion whatsoever. Quake didn't know if that meant yes or no. "So what did your source say and who the hell is your source?" Jarlath said, spinning back around in his comfortable black, plush leather seat to face Quake Man.

"She works at this bar called Jacob."

"She, she who?"

"Well this girl I have been messing with for some time now. Her name is Kila. She said that Alayne and some young, pregnant girl were there. Kila thought that it was a little strange for Alayne to be at that bar so she called me and let me know, only because she was concerned though. You know that bar is like a hole in the wall. A girl with Alayne's status shouldn't be in such a bar. When I called you, you never answered so I told her to follow her to make sure that nothing happened to Alayne. Kila followed them outside by the trash cans. That's when I thought it was a little strange."

"So you were on the phone when she followed Alayne out to the trash cans?"

"Yeah, I wanted to make sure I heard everything. Just in case somebody tried to sneak up on Kila listening to them. Anyway, Alayne was telling the girl that you were going to kill her because she was pregnant. I couldn't understand why because I couldn't hear too good, but I do know that she said that you were going to kill her and that you were a dangerous man and some more shit that wasn't too cool man."

Jarlath just sat in his seat, still showing no emotions.

"So I had the boys follow Alayne for a couple of days. You know, just so I can have my facts right when I came to you and that's when I found her talking to Ronny at that famous spaghetti joint. I don't know what's going on man but that nigga trying to set you up for real."

"Ronny is a man who can't take losing well. He never had what it took to be a man in power and couldn't take that conclusion lying down. It was more of his dream to be an Illuminati leader than mine, but the men on board didn't think he had the qualities, so they chose me. Ever since then, he has become obsessed with making me pay for betraying him."

"Betraying him? How were you betraying him because they chose you?"

"We made a promise to each other that we wouldn't accept if both of us didn't get accepted. But I knew better than that. Ronny was too hungry for power. As soon as he would have gotten the position, he would've had me killed. So I took the position, not that I had a choice anyway. Ronny became my enemy from that point on. I could have done the same thing to him. You know, had him killed, but I didn't. Instead I saved him from the board. They wanted to do him in as soon as I took leadership. They said that he would cause problems for the society because he wasn't accepted."

"I mean, I know y'all go way back Jarlath but you know the line was right man. You should have silenced him a long time ago. Why didn't you?"

"Because I promised the first out of the two girls I ever loved that I wouldn't."

"What that got to do with knocking him off?"

"She was his sister."

"I never knew you and Aleesa were involved."

"Nobody did. I couldn't speak on it at the time because of safety issues. I told her I would make sure nothing happened to her brother. Only If I knew her life was going to end the way it did, I wouldn't have made that promise."

"Yea, that was messed up what happened to her." Quake Man bowed his head and shook it looking at the desk for a second.

"You don't know the half of it." Jarlath spun in his chair glancing at his view before turning back to face Quake Man.

"So what are we going to do about this nigga, Jarlath? I'm about fed up with him. This guy is using everybody for bait. I mean, dang, Kilo didn't have nothing to do with this shit man. Ronny's just stepping on any and everybody to get to the top. He doesn't care. You know we got to break that promise now. Oh, and I'm sorry I had to tell you about Alayne, man. I know that must hurt a little bit. Her being the second girl you gave your heart to and all."

Jarlath cracked a smile. "I never said that she was the second girl to have my heart."

"Oh, I really never seen you get too serious with anybody else so I guess I just assumed. Who was the second one then?"

"The young, pregnant girl you seen Alayne talking to."

Quake Man was completely confused and Jarlath left him that way. Jarlath walked to his front door, opening it for Quake Man to exit.

"Don't worry about Ronny, I will handle him. This one is personal plus, I wouldn't send a boy to do a man's job. Ronny is no small fish in the pond. He is a dangerous man, just not dangerous enough. Tell no one about this conversation. Not even my precious wife. As a matter of fact, keep following her. Don't let her out your eyesight. If she sneezes wrong, I want to know about it."

"You got it Jarlath, man. Let me know if there's anything else you need, you know I'm here."

"I know Quake, I got you. Stay posted and remember don't tell nobody anything. The littlest hole can sink the ship."

"Okay." Quake walked out of the office with his head held up high and pants bagged low.

αααα

"What was so important that you had to call me three times? I told you, you can't be calling me like that. I do have a husband, you know?"

"Yeah, yeah."

"I'm serious with your ass Ronny, don't yeah, yeah me."

"Trust me sweetheart, your husband is not worrying about you. He got another butterfly on his mind."

"Yeah, the same one who got you wrapped around her hands."

"Look I didn't call you here for all that. Did you do what I asked you to do?"

"What you ask me to do, Ronny?"

"Don't play with me, Alayne. Did you plant the shit or what?"

"Yes, damn, why you all uptight and shit?" Alayne got up from the bar and walked towards the patio. "Because I don't have time for mistakes, Alayne, and you better not be fucking me." Ronny turned Alayne around, holding on tight to her right arm.

"First of all, watch your damn mouth and let my damn arm go. Alayne demanded snatching away from Ronny. I am not one of your little girls who you boss around. If I said I planted the shit, I planted the shit. Now I'm hungry and you're going to sit down and have something to eat with me."

"I don't have time, Alayne."

"I don't want to hear that junk, Ronny. You shouldn't call me out of my spa treatment when you could have asked me that on the phone."

"I told you I don't talk business over the phone." Alayne pulled up a chair next to the tall green and purple flowers. She wanted to watch the New York traffic while she enjoyed her meal. Ronny checked his surroundings then his phone for missed calls while Alayne stared at the menu in silent. "Are you two ready to order?"

"Yes we are. I will have the chicken Caesar salad and a glass of grape wine." Alayne said.

"Um, you can give me the steak and loaded baked potato with sour cream, cheese, bacon, and chili and a sweet tea."

"Sure, will this be on one ticket, sir, or two?"

"You can just put it on one." Ronny handed the waitress the menu.

"Oh look at you, so you do know how to be a gentleman?" Alayne smiled from ear-to-ear as she teased Ronny.

"Sometimes, I guess," Ronny responded, blushing.

"Ronny, have you visited Alessa's grave site?"

"Nope, I don't think she will agree with me being there. She didn't approve of my lifestyle. She didn't care for the violence."

"Oh, I'm sure she has forgiven you by now Ronny."

"I'm gonna have to disagree with you."

"Here is your tea, sir, and your wine, ma'am," the young, black waitress said interrupting their conversation. Alayne continued the conversation watching the waitress walk away.

"You can't beat yourself up about it Ronny."

"So you telling me you would've forgiven me for taking your life just because I'm your brother."

Alayne choked on her smooth grape wine. She knew nothing about Ronny killing his sister. "Damn Ronny you sacrificed your sister for this bullshit life, man?"

Ronny was silent for about ten seconds. He thought she already knew. "Yes I did, I regretted it the moment I did it. I so badly wanted to bring her back, but I couldn't and for years, her death has haunted me. That's why I can't fail. I have come this far; I must get what it is I want out of life. I have sacrificed too much. If I could bring her back, then I would walk away from it all but I can't. I was young and stupid so I refuse to let her death be for no reason."

Alayne twirled her wine in the glass, looking off into space. "The things people do for power, boy, I tell you. Well, anyway I did what you asked. I am through with you. Don't call me no more." Alayne drunk the rest of her wine and walked off on Ronny. She didn't even wait for her salad. Her last words before leaving Ronny were, "I wish you all the luck and bad luck you deserve. I hope the power you are craving for is worth it, because from where I'm sitting, I got to tell you, it's not."

αααα

"Hello."

"Hey Zakiya, um, what you doing?" Saran asked sounding down.

"I'm reading, why?" Zakiya sat her book down in her lap and held the phone closer to her to her ear. She wanted to hear everything.

"Because I got something to tell you as usual."

"I'm guessing the news is not good."

"Your guess is right, genius. Kelly said that she was having a salad at Naomie Restaurant and she saw Khalon there having some drink with some lady."

"Oh, okay, don't worry about it; it's probably the lady he said he has been working with on this case."

"Oooooh okay, good. I would have hated it to be anything else. Shoot, I haven't used my forty five in a minute."

Zakiya laughed at Saran's joke. "Okay girl, let me get back into this book. I will call you back."

"Okay Zakiya."

TILL DEATH DO US APART

Khalon ran into the house, slamming the door and looking behind him, paying Zakiya no attention. Zakiya sat on the sofa rocking Naira to sleep. "Khalon, why do you look so jumpy?"

Khalon double backed to the living room. "Oh, I'm sorry baby; I have to use the bathroom bad." Khalon kissed Naira on the forehead and continued running up the stairs.

"Please with the noise Khalon I'm trying to put Naira to sleep!" Zakiya yelled up the stairs to where Khalon was making noise moving things. Khalon ignored Zakiya and continued making the loud noise.

Zakiya took Naira to the nursery to lay her down and went to the master bedroom to see what Khalon was doing. "Are you okay in here?"

Khalon walked towards Zakiya, turning her around at the door, pressing his manhood against her butt and kissing all over her neck. "Can I have you for dinner, Miss Lady?"

"Oh no, my mother said I can't do that until I'm married," Zakiya said, joking around with the man whom she never had sex with.

He turned Zakiya loose and bent down on one knee, and out of nowhere he demanded, "Well marry me, Ms.Kiya,"

"What did you say, Khalon?" Zakiya asked with her hands on her hips.

"Will you marry me? Add the icing on the cake. Give me the key to my lock. Ms. Zakiya, will you complete me?"

Zakiya's hands went from her hips to her face. She couldn't believe what Khalon was asking her. "Oh my God! Are you serious! Yes, I will marry you, man! Yes!"

Khalon placed the ring that he made so much noise looking for on Zakiya's finger.

"OMG! It's so big. This thing must cost a fortune."

"You can't put a price on love. Now listen I got Saran coming by, she is going to watch baby Naira for us. I got a whole day planned for us before you go back to work."

"I don't know if I'm ready to leave her with somebody, Khalon. You know she is still very young. How about we just stay here and veg out in front of the TV?" Zakiya flopped down on the bed.

"You know I would love to do that, but I already paid for everything. Khalon walked towards Zakiya standing in front of her pleading his case. Just trust me, please. Besides Saran is Naira's God momma. She's just not anybody. I have been looking forward to this day all week."

Zakiya stood up and grabbed Khalon's hands. "Okay, I guess. Since you went through all that trouble to plan whatever it is that you have planned." Muah! Khalon lips were smooth and moist. "I love you, Muah!" Zakiya kissed Khalon once more, this time on his cheeks before walking to her closet.

The wardrobe Zakiya had stashed at Khalon house was new and purchased by him. She purposely left her clothes at her apartment just in case it didn't work out living together. Khalon followed Zakiya to the closet with papers in his hand.

"Baby, can you sign these papers for me?"

"What are they, baby?" Zakiya took the papers out of Khalon hands glancing through them.

"House insurance, car insurance, stuff like that. I need to put you and Naira on my insurance just in case of any accidents. Now that y'all are going to be

196

a new addition to my family. It's time for me to renew and I wanted to make sure that y'all be taken care of in case anything happens to me." Without reading, Zakiya signed the papers, trusting Khalon's words.

αααα

Khalon was dressed in a gray piped tuxedo, paired with casual gray sneakers. His dreads were wrapped back around his head and his body was finger licking good. Zakiya could barely believe that he was her fiancé-- not that she didn't look equally as good as he did. The Versace pre-fall frock fit the new mother perfectly, the beautifully embellished bodice accentuating her curves. The two smelled like a mixture of lovely flowers.

"Are you ready, my love?" Khalon asked, giving Zakiya his arm to grab.

"Yes, my king." Zakiya grabbed Khalon's arm and the two walked down the stairs like they were on the way to their senior prom.

"Aw, you two look so beautiful, y'all make me want to go out and find my Prince Charming. You don't have no brothers, do you Khalon?"

Khalon and Zakiya laughed while still holding each other tightly. "Nawl, I don't Saran but don't worry as beautiful as you are, you will not be waiting too long."

"Aw, see, don't you just know how to say the right stuff to a girl. Now like an over protective momma, I want some pictures of you two. So smile like your last name was Gates."

Khalon and Zakiya took three pictures feeling higher than the clouds.

"Now are you sure you can handle Naira?"

"Yes, girl I got her."

197

"I pumped out some breast milk in the refrigerator; it should be enough to last until I get back. It's in the container that reads BM. If she gets too fussy, hold her close to your chest and rock her and don't do no rock the cradle type moves on my baby."

Saran and Khalon burst out laughing at Zakiya who was acting like an over protective mother. "She uses the bathroom a lot so make sure you keep her dry. Her diapers are upstairs in her night stand. Let me see, am I missing anything? All the numbers to get in touch with me are posted on the refrigerator as well."

"Girl if you don't leave already with all these damn rules and carrying on..."

"Come on neat freak, she got it. We need to make our reservations because this place stays packed." Khalon grabbed Zakiya's hip, leading her out the front door.

"FREEZE! HOLD YOUR HANDS UP!" the captain of the New York police department screamed out to Khalon and Zakiya. Khalon's front yard was covered with S.W.A.T. Zakiya was completely confused. Until she saw Jarlath get out of the car.

"You have the wrong guy. He is a detective. It's him you are looking for," Zakiya said, pointing at Jarlath. Zakiya's first thoughts were that Jarlath got to the police and told them something to make them believe that Khalon was a murderer or some type of criminal. With so many connections in his pockets, anything was possible.

"Khalon, it's over with. Put your hands on your head." Captain Johnson demanded.

"Zakiya, I am Captain Johnson. Don't make a move, okay?"

Zakiya stood with her hands in the air, scared out of her mind. Saran watched out the window, scared to make a move.

"He is not the man you think he is Zakiya," the captain assured Zakiya.

Khalon took a good look at Zakiya and kissed her on the cheeks. "I love you and I'm sorry for any pain I may have cost you. Just know I never loved anyone the way I loved you." Khalon took the gun out of his pockets and placed it to his head.

TWISTED SECRETS

"Ronny put the gun down now!" "Don't do this." Captain Johnson screamed out.

"I'm not going to jail Captain, I'm just not," Khalon screamed. Khalon was acting like a deranged man, pacing with the gun to his head. "It's over Ronny, its over!" Captain Johnson gun followed Khalon's every move.

Confused, Zakiya grabbed her hair, then shook her head, watching Khalon go insane. Her mind wasn't digesting the drama quick enough and before she could calm herself her body begins to shake uncontrollably. Zakiya looked like she was having a seizure standing. She couldn't believe her eyes and ears. The man who she thought she knew was a complete stranger. Tears started to roll out her eyes and down her face like a lint brush on black jeans.

"What did you do Khalon? What have you done?" she screams at him unable to fight back her tears. "Who the hell are you?"

Khalon turned to Zakiya with the gun still aimed at his head. "A man that found peace with you, a man who loves you dearly."

"Then put the gun down, Khalon."

"I can't, we could never be happily-ever-after together. I have done too many things that will prevent that from ever happening. I just want you to know I love you with all of my heart."

Jarlath walked closer to Khalon and Zakiya. "You just had to have it all, didn't you? If you break her heart, I will hunt you down," Khalon said to Jarlath as he walked closer to the porch where Zakiya and Khalon were standing.

"I feel no remorse for you. Go ahead do us all a favor, Ronny, because if you don't, you will be a dead man walking. I'm going to make sure of it. Your life will be one miserable wreck, I promise." Captain Johnson walked towards both Khalon and Jarlath slowly with his gun steady. "I will put a bullet in the next motherfucka who moves, don't move. Jarlath took one more step towards Khalon.

"Jarlath, stand back now!" the captain screamed.

The S.W.A.T. were in position to take a shot at Khalon if he made one false move, but now they had to aim at Jarlath as well. They weren't sure on his intentions. Before anyone could make another move Khalon blew his brains out, right in front of Zakiya. She screamed, still shaking uncontrollably, breaking down to her knees and crying her eyes out with blood all over her white Chanel blouse. Saran who was still watching through the window broke down into tears too, crying so loud Jarlath could hear her on the porch.

Jarlath wanted to hold Zakiya badly, but he knew that she was brainwashed by Ronny. She still didn't know who he really was and in her eyes he was a good man while Jarlath was the monster. It took a lot for Jarlath to put his desires to the side to do what any real man with a heart would do, allowed her time to moan for the man she loved. Leaving her bent down on her knees crying her eyes out, Jarlath walked away from the porch and jumped in his black

Navigator. Zakiya took one last look at Khalon with her blouse covering her nose. She could smell the scent of his scattered brains. Tears poured out of her eyes as she watched the coroner zip Khalon up in the body bag.

"Excuse me, captain," Zakiya with static in her voice. "Are you going to allow me to give him a proper burial?"

Captain Johnson was still in shock of the news himself. Khalon a.k.a. Ronny had him fooled as well. He looked at Khalon like a son. They grew very fond of each other. Khalon was named one of his best detectives and now that this was out, the captain was going have to look into all of the cases he ever did. The Captain agreed to give Khalon a proper burial because he just couldn't believe that everything about him was lie. It was just too hard to swallow. Plus Captain Johnson knew if he was brain washed by Khalon that Zakiya had to be as well. He couldn't begin to image what she had to be feeling.

Captain Johnson grabbed Zakiya by the shoulders with his two hands and said, "Yea, I wouldn't have it any other way. Once I'm through with him, he is all yours."

Zakiya's tears once again began to roll down her face. She sat on the porch and watched as the coroner and police made her house a crime scene.

αααα

After a whole month, Zakiya was able to go back to the house. She honored Khalon by giving him a beautiful funeral and a large tombstone with his real name carved into it, reading, R.I.P. Khalon you will forever be remembered. Zakiya made herself believe that Khalon wanted to change, the person he was with her, was the man he always wanted to be deep down inside. There were a handful of people there which surprised her because she figured she would be the only one there. Ms. White and a few officers, and she even saw Alayne who apologized deeply to her. The house felt empty without Khalon but Zakiya made it her business to go back.

"Saran, did you get Naira's bag out of the car?" Zakiya asked Saran who agreed to help her with Naira while she sorted out things in the house.

"Yeah, I got it. It's right here." Saran sat at the dinette table with Zakiya who was reading over the papers Khalon made her sign before killing himself.

"Thank you. You know you have been a tremendous help. I don't know if I could have made it this far without you by my side." Zakiya's tears blurred her vision. She quickly she wiped them, then she stood up for a brief second to hug Saran tight.

"You don't have to thank me girl, you been just as good to me as I am to you. Zakiya assured Saran. I mean the money I'm making with you is satisfying and you have never treated me like an employee without a face. Not to mention the friendship we have established. Saran couldn't help herself. She expressed her feelings to Zakiya even though she knew Zakiya hated being emotional. I feel like I have a family now and that's what families do. They stick together no matter what. They have each other's back. I mean just look how far we have come since the first time we met. You basically have grown into a lovely, young lady."

Zakiya's tears doubled. "I'm sorry. I'm trying not to cry because I'm tired of crying but you know you're right. We have come far since the first time we met and this is not the end. We are going to go even further, baby. Trust me."

"Oh trust me, I do. You are one ambitious young lady, honey. You are so ambitious I get motivated just by looking at you. I guess that's why I enjoy your company because you are so real. You just going through a little turbulence right now but don't worry. The fight is almost over and we should be arriving to paradise soon."

"Ooh I like that," Zakiya said as she wiped the tears off her face. "Girl, Khalon left me three million dollars, all three of his cars, and this house."

Saran's eyes widened and her mouth dropped open. "Are you serious?"

"Yes, I'm dead serious. He tricked me and said that these were insurance papers but he signed everything over to me. The house alone is worth 2.3 million. He even left his restaurant and club in my name. It was like he knew he was going to kill himself."

"Do you know the story behind everything yet?"

"No, I have been prolonging, but I am going to find out."

ααα α

"Thank you, Jarlath. I know I haven't always been the nicest person to you but it's not in me to ignore the good in a person when I see it. You just never really showed it to me. I guess that was a problem on my behalf because I knew that my son had good taste in people. So if he trusted you enough to hang with you, then I should have been more open to you." Ms. White sat down on her sofa sipping her ice cold homemade lemonade.

"It's not your fault. I never tried to show you the good in me because then I would feel like I'm trying to convince you of something. I like to know people's opinion about me without them knowing me sometimes. I get to see what I look like on the outside but I was never mad at you Ms. White.

"I just can't believe it. That man came to my house and had me eating out of the palms of his hands even though I knew he was always the troubled kid in the neighborhood."

"You just wanted to see good in him, Ms. White, like you wanted to see it in all of us."

"Well, I didn't call you here to get all down you. I just wanted to say thank you for keeping your word even though I was so mean to you. You even came to tell me in person. You know the day he killed himself?" Ms. White twirled her index finger in circular motion.

"Yea, I know." Jarlath nodded his head.

"I was beyond rude to you and I just have to say I am so sorry, baby. I apologize."

Ms. White walked over to the chair that Jarlath was sitting in and hugged him. He stood to his feet accepting the old lady's hug and apology. "Thank you, that mean a lot to me." Jarlath gave Ms. White a respectable peck on the cheeks.

"Now you stay out of trouble. I don't want to see you in nobody's newspaper. I think if I have to go to another one of you boy's funeral, I will lose the little faith I do have."

"Oh you don't have to worry about that Ms. White, not at all. I'm going to die of natural causes."

Ms. White burst out laughing, breaking the sad spell. "I hear you. I'm going to hold you to that too."

"Okay, you do that," Jarlath said as he walked out of Ms. White's front door. "Ms. White if you ever need anything, don't hesitate to call. A ride to the store, money, company, anything, you feel free to call, you hear?"

"I hear you, son. I will do just that."

αααα

"Oh yeah, I forgot I had this." Zakiya grabbed the skirt off the rack holding it up to her waist, looking at herself in the mirror. The large walk in closet was full of designers and Zakiya could never just walk in and pick an outfit out. After a long consideration, Zakiya slid on her Costa skirt and blouse combo with her Walter Steiger satin pumps and headed down stairs. Before leaving out the door she asked, "Saran are you sure you going to be okay here?"

Throwing her hand in the free air Saran answered, "Girl, come back with some answers then I will be okay."

Obeying Saran's command for the first time, Zakiya stormed out the door speeding to Jarlath's office.

αααα

"She is here Boss." The receptionist spoke to Jarlath through an office camera.

"Thank you, send her up." Jarlath watched Zakiya coming up the elevator on his office camera and

as soon as she opened the door he said to her, "I thought you would never come. He stood by the window looking out at the city secretly thanking God for the opportunity to speak to Zakiya again. How are you holding up?" Jarlath turned to face Zakiya and the two eyes meet. Quickly, Zakiya held her head down seating in his chair, leaving the guess chair available for him.

"I'm doing okay, I guess, for now. I want to know..." Zakiya hesitated, taking a deep breath before completing her sentence. "I want to know what happened."

Jarlath sat in the guest chair, looking Zakiya straight in the eye. "Are you sure?"

"Yes, I'm sure. I feel that's the only way I'm going to have closure."

Jarlath sat back in the chair with his hands pressed together, looking at Zakiya breathing deeply. After three minutes, he began. "Khalon a.k.a. Ronny was a friend of mine growing up. We parted and became enemies when my position in life grew higher than his. Some people we both knew and respected played a trick on him, telling him if he sacrificed his sister's life then he could join our forces. He made the choice to kill his sister and then blamed me for it. He said I knew that they were lying to him but I knew nothing about the charade until the end. The thing was, if he killed his sister, the love of my life, then he could have my place in the Society."

"So you were in love with his sister?"

"Yelp, the first girl out of the two I have ever loved. Anyway, Ronny, I mean Khalon, has been trying to nail things on me ever since. That's why he killed Kilo so that he could set me up for the murder."

Confused, Zakiya threw both her hands in the air and asked, "Then where do I come in at?"

Closing his eyes for two seconds rubbing his chin, Jarlath took a deep breath and said, "You are the second girl I have ever loved."

Zakiya swallowed the mouthful of saliva that watered up in her mouth.

"He figured if he had you on his team for bait then the plan wouldn't go wrong. It was him that had the men following you and knocking at your door. Him and my ex-wife Alayne was in on it together. She was pissed at me because he convinced her that I was the one who killed Kilo and her and Kilo were secret lovers. He convinced her that I killed Kilo because she was seeing him and she convinced you that I was after you because you were pregnant with my daughter, who by the way I would love to see."

Zakiya shook her head. "This is going to take some time to soak in. Well, I must say I owe you an apology. I should have never kept our daughter away from you. She is three months now and her name is Naira. She looks just like you. I don't know if it was because I couldn't stand you when I was carrying her or if you just had strong genes, but she is definitely your daughter and you are more than welcome to see her at any time."

Zakiya wanted to lighten the mood up because she was sick and tired of being sad. "So what you going to do for me, if I let you see your daughter?"

Jarlath laughed. "Oh, okay I see. What do you want, Miss Lady?"

Zakiya walked over to Jarlath's seat and stood him up on his feet. "I want to get to know you, Mister," Zakiya said, taking Jarlath's hands and wrapping them around her small but mature waist.

"Sure." Jarlath took Zakiya's face and pressed it to his, not letting up on the long passionate kiss. He ended his kiss with soft pecks on her sweet lips, then placing nice wet ones on her favorite spot, the neck. "I love you girl more than you know."

"I guess I just got to catch up with you then."

"Do you think maybe we can do it while being joined to one another?"

Zakiya was offered her second engagement in one year. Overwhelmed was an understatement for her. "Are you asking me to be your wife?"

"Yes, if you will have me. No, if you are not ready for marriage."

Zakiya laughed at Jarlath. "You just can't stand the word no being in the same sentence as your name, could you?"

While Zakiya was talking, Jarlath did something out of the ordinary. He bent down on one knee with Zakiya's left hand in his right. "Will you be the sun to my day, hype to my night, my better half? Zakiya Rivers, will you marry me?"

Zakiya wanted to cry but for a good reason this time. Jarlath was about to be hers. Did he just call me Zakiya Rivers? Zakiya asked herself. "I got to say my name sounds good coming out your mouth like that. Yes, guy, I will marry you."

Zakiya's tears dripped on Jarlath knuckles. She tried to wipe them off, but Jarlath said, "Leave it. I did not tell you to clean my hand."

Unable to control themselves the two kissed again. For over ten minutes, the two were glued together. "I'm so looking forward to my life with you, Zakiya. I never thought that the day would come when I would look forward to a future with a white picket fence."

Zakiya giggled like a high school girl with a crush. "Well, life has its way of shaking things up. You know throwing in shocking surprises. Who knows we might even be the modern day Cosby's."

Jarlath smiled at the thought of having a family to grow old with. "I hope you know what you are getting yourself into because I'm never divorcing you once we marry. It will be to death do us part, but I assure you it will be nothing less than exciting. So you won't have to worry about getting bored or having to dip out on me."

"Jarlath, I take vows seriously. There will be no dipping out once I say the words I do. You are going to be the last man I touch for the rest of my life and I'm cool with that. Just keep me happy and always respect me."

Jarlath's heart warmed up as he listened to Zakiya talk about the future they were to share together. "That's not hard to do. Is that all? is there any other wish you would like?"

"No, I don't need too many things Jarlath. Just you, that's enough for me, although I enjoy the riches, fabulous clothes, nice jewelry, and expensive shoes like the next diva. My life will not stop if I didn't get them though."

"I forgot how mature you are. How I felt so comfortable around you. You make it so easy for me to be me, Zakiya. That's how I know I am going to enjoy being your other half and no, I don't think things will be just perfect because no human, relationship, or marriage is. But we are going to aim as close to it as we can." Jarlath opened his office door leading the way out and Zakiya followed.

"I will call you when I get home." Muah. Zakiya couldn't help herself she kissed Jarlath once more. "I have to go relieve Saran. She is watching Naira."

After kissing Zakiya back twice Jarlath offered, "I can come with you if you want?"

"No, I don't need you to see me scream when I tell Saran the great news. Then there are my folks who I have to tell as well. Don't worry, you going have the rest of your life to spend with me." The two kissed again before Zakiya continued out the door.

Zakiya jumped in her black Range Rover, reminiscing on the last time she was excited to be married. Then she thought about how quick it went sour, out of nowhere she begins to pray. "Lord I thank you for blessing me with love again and I ask if you could please bless me with a long and healthy marriage. Crossing her fingers was the only thing

Zakiya could do to relax and not stress about her future with Jarlath. If things went wrong for her and Jarlath, she wouldn't be able to take it. Zakiya realized that she never stopped caring for Jarlath. Things started to make sense to her finally.

"Maybe God sent me Khalon to show me how good of a man Jarlath really is, because God knows if I never met Khalon, I would have still thought that Jarlath was a man who only cared for himself. I guess sometimes all smiles can mean disaster and silence can mean greatness. I never saw Khalon for a bad person because his smiles were too bright. I didn't know what to suspect from him, unlike Jarlath, who puts it all on the table. The gospel music Zakiya had playing down low in the truck had her thinking. . "Yeah, life for me just has to be great here on out. I can't see it any other way. I won't see it no other way," Zakiya talked to herself as she sat in the New York traffic.

HAPPILY-EVER–AFTER/NOT

Three years later

"You are glowing, young lady. Are we expecting someone new?" Saran asked Zakiya who was humming Beyonce's "Smash Into You."

"No we are not. I'm not ready for anymore at the moment. Hell, Naira is a handful but I am happy Saran. I feel like I'm on cloud nine. I mean it's kind of scary when I think about it because who do you know gets everything they ask for?"

Saran looked at Zakiya for thirty long seconds and said, "You my friend, you."

It felt surreal to Zakiya. C had everything she ever asked for, from a healthy baby girl, to a loyal friend, to a great man. Zakiya even looked at her bad dreams about Khalon blowing his brains out in front of her as a blessing because anytime she had the bad dreams, Jarlath would hold her all night rubbing his hands freely through her thick rich black hair, soothing her, assuring her that things were going be alright. "I guess you right Saran and while we are on the subject, I just want to say I am so thankful to have you as a friend. You have been a girl's rock. I don't know how long I would have been able to make it here in this crazy city without you."

"We have helped each other honey. I remembered when you was just a little girl, now look at you, all old enough to buy a drink and everything." The girls both burst out into laugher at the fact that they were acting as if they had really gotten old.

"I know one thing. You better have fun for me too. C time you sip a margarita, you better sip twice." Saran added rolling her eyes.

"I will not. You trying to get me drunk so Jarlath can take advantage of me, but I tell you what. You can take your own drink when you go."

Saran looked at Zakiya with a surprise face. "Say what now?"

Zakiya pulled out two first class tickets to Brazil. "Boo Yaa! You are going to Brazil chick."

Saran took the tickets out of Zakiya's hands, looking at them closely. she needed to feel the tickets to know it was real.

"Of course, you can't go until me and Jarlath get back from Paris but you are definitely going, honey."

"Aww, thank you, Zakiya, you are the best."

"I know," Zakiya said quickly without thinking.

"I know you want to go out and see the world too and I have no problem with helping you do so. I mean you do so much for me and Naira. You are my best friend, chick, and like I said, I'm glad to have you in my life. You have really been a big help."

Saran walked over to Zakiya before she could even get 'big help' out good and hugged her tight, kissing her all on the cheeks.

"Get off me lady," Zakiya jokingly said.

"You gonna have so much fun in Paris, Ms.Thing."

"I know. It's the last trip I am taking as Zakiya Williams. Very soon, you will be friends with a married woman." Zakiya tooted her lips while smiling.

"I can't wait to that date comes. Hell, you've been holding it off long enough. A sister been done rolled over in her grave before you say the words 'I DO.'" Saran added.

Zakiya's heart started racing like she was about to have a heart attack. "Don't say stuff like that Saran, Why would you play like that, that's just not funny," Zakiya said with a loud pitch.

Saran looked at Zakiya who was pacing the kitchen floor throwing the can goods that she just recently bought in the cabinets. She walked over to her, holding her tight. "Calm down girl, nothing is going to happen to you or me. You scared of your blessings to the point you're running, you not being able to enjoy them. Just accept the fact that good things happen to good people. Shit as much as you and your momma pray, you shouldn't even be surprised that you are loaded with blessing. You so scared that something is going to go wrong that you are forgetting to enjoy everything that is going right."

Zakiya tried to catch her tears before it hit Saran's shoulders but she failed. "I'm sorry, you're right. I got to stop tripping. It's just I got this feeling that something is about to happen and every time I try to shake it, it comes right back."

"Nothing is about to happen Zakiya, you just scared of your happiness. I want you to go to Paris and just relax, live, and love, girl. You deserve it."

Zakiya nodded her head yes and wiped her tears. Saran always knew what to say whenever Zakiya was freaking about something which made Zakiya feel even more blessed to have her. Like clockwork, Jarlath walked in the door with his baby girl Naira in his arms. Zakiya gathered herself together she straightened out her clothes, and tried to fix her voice back to happy rather than scared.

"I swear if I didn't know her, I would think she couldn't walk," Zakiya said to Jarlath as he walked towards her to get his afternoon kiss.

"Well she can, she just don't have to, MUAH." The kiss was wet and soft and both Zakiya and Jarlath looked forward to it every day.

"Hey Mommy."

"Hey baby girl, how was your day?" Zakiya asked Naira as she took her from her father's arms and embraced her in hers.

"It was fun. I wrote my name today and we made Christmas cookies."

"Y'all did?"

"Yes, and I made you and Daddy a gift, but you can't get it until Christmas."

"Okay, well go put it under the tree."

"Momma, is I'm still going to Grandma house for the break?"

"No Naira we have a change of plans. Grandma has finally decided to take a trip, so she will be going on a cruise for the Christmas break."

Naira poked her lips out, tilted her head to the side while her beautiful brown eyes sparkled. "But Mommy, you said I could go to Grandma's house. Everyone is going to be on a trip but me," the three year old said clearly.

"Grandma needs this trip, she never gets out of Jackson so don't be selfish. When Dad and I come back, you, me, and him are going to take a trip of our own. Anywhere you want to go."

"Anywhere?" Naira asked with both her hands pressed together under her chin with her head to the side.

"Yes, anywhere, Naira." Zakiya knew the exact place Naira had in mind when she repeated anywhere "Disney World."

"Daddy, you hear this right?"

Jarlath who tried his hardest to stay out of Naira and her mother's agreement nodded his head. "Of course, princess."

By the time Jarlath came home, Zakiya already had her and Jarlath's luggage packed and posted at the door ready to go.

"John, get the bags in the car," Jarlath said to his muscle."

"Now you better be a good girl, Naira. I don't want Aunt Saran to call me with bad news, you hear me?" Zakiya had Naira's chin in her hand.

"Yes Mommy."

"Now give me kiss. MUAH."

"Aunt Saran, are you ready for an adventure?"

Saran shook her head. She knew she was in for a ride. Naira could stay up all night if you let her. "Yes ma'am, I am, but first I think it's time for a nap. Then we can talk about the adventures later because a tired kid makes a cranky kid."

Naira knew it was coming. C always took naps when she got home from school. Zakiya said her last goodbyes before leaving.

"Alright you two, we about to head out, I love yall. Saran make sure you call, and make sure your phone is not on vibrate because if I call and don't get you, I will freak out."

"Please turn that phone off vibrate. I will hate for her to freak out while we're gone," Jarlath added, showing his almost never seen humor.

"I got you, I got you. Now stop worrying and go, go for goodness sake!" Saran pushed on Zakiya's back shoving her out the door. "Bye! Call me when yall make it. Yall know the longer the two of you stand here the longer it's going to take for Miss Naira to find the zzz's."

Both Zakiya and Jarlath laughed as they walked quickly out the door jumping into the backseat of Jarlath's Maybach.

αααα

"Can you read me another bedtime story, Saran, please?" Naira pleaded, looking up at Saran with her beautiful, brown eyes.

"I just read you two, baby girl, besides you need to get some sleep. We got a big day tomorrow remember."

"Oh yeah that's right. I got to get rested for the Nutcracker tomorrow." Naira snuggled with her brown bear Teddy tucked in her arms squeezing him tight.

"Goodnight Naira."

"Goodnight Saran."

Saran had been up all day playing with Naira because she only napped for thirty minutes and then she was back at it again. Saran was ready to kick up her feet, drink some wine, and fall asleep to some slow jams.

On her way to the kitchen, she heard small voices as if they were coming from the back side of the house. Saran walked down the flared staircase towards the kitchen window to see if she could see anyone since all the lights were off except the ones in the sitting area. In the dark, Saran was able to see a man in a black balaclava mask with holes only for the mouth and eyes. Immediately Saran dropped to the floor and so did her heart that was beating a hundred miles per minute. There was no phone in sight and before Saran could even crawl to the house phone, gunfire was shot throughout the house.

217

From each window, bullets entered. All Saran could see was fire lighting up the dark. All Saran could do was scream at the top of her lungs, shaking scared for her and Naira's life. She tried crawling back up the stair case, but she didn't make it too far. The black masks were twenty deep and they were everywhere. It was like a gangsta movie only it was happening for real.

The 6'2" built baritone voiced guy said to Saran, "Where you think you going, bitch?" Before Saran could answer, the guy shot her five times, three in the back, one in the head, and one in the leg. Saran laid soaked in her blood and loose bowl movement with one tear rolling down her face.

The men destroyed the house breaking china, busting the mounted plasmas, smashing the very expensive wine bottles. "Man fuck all that, find the little girl so we can go!" the baritone voice yelled to the rest of the clan.

"Man where those cameras at?" The husky guy asked with his deep voice. I know this man got cameras hid in here somewhere."

"Man fuck the camera, I want him to see who we are."

"I don't know, man, if that's a good idea, just think Rrrr…"

"Man, shut your stuttering fat ass up and don't say my motherfucking name. Is you stupid?"

The boy obeyed the demand and walked off. It was hard for him to get his words out so he just left it alone but he knew that the wrong woman had been killed and someone was going have to pay when they returned.

The leader of the clan ran upstairs and went straight to Naira's room as if he had been there before. Naira hid under her bed shaking with tears flowing down her face. Her heart was beating so fast she could hardly breathe.

"Come little girl, wherever you are."

Naira tried to hold in her cries but she couldn't. She began to cry loudly and he snatched her right up, throwing her over his shoulders as he ran down the stairs and out the house to the black SUVs where the rest waited.

Naira screamed, kicked, and scratched but there was nothing she could do with the strong man. "Stop kicking me little girl or I'm going to let my dog bite you."

Terrified of big dogs, Naira stopped fighting and the unknown monster placed a black cotton pillowcase over her head, with two holes cut out vertical for her nose and mouth. "Man we killed the wrong girl that was not his wife."

"Didn't I tell you to shut your fat ass up? That was his wife."

"Ask the theeeee, the, little girrrrrl then."

"I ain't got to. Now shut up about it. What you trying to give her hints or something!" Niara jumped at the loud deep voice. I want my daddy, where is mommy? I hope the monster big dog don't bite me. Naira thought to herself as she sighed silently. You could see her lips crinkled through the hole as tears rolled down her face beneath the pillow case. She crossed her fingers behind her back praying to God for her momma. Please God let mommy find me, please let my mommy find me.

To Be
Continued

COMING SOON!

THE KING'S REVENGE"

SPEECHLESS

"Muah, Muah." Zakiya trailed Jarlath's body with soft moist kisses down his chest, stopping at his penis, slurping in a mouthful, leaving no air in her jaws.

"Aww," Jarlath moaned. "Put it all in, put it all in baby. Damn, I love that shit."

Zakiya and Jarlath's flight was delayed so they decided to get a room instead of returning home and having to say bye to Naira again. Zakiya and Jarlath both hated being away from her but they were due for some alone time.

Zakiya shoved as much as Jarlath's mandingo in her mouth as she could. She enjoyed making love to him. The love she felt for him was bigger than sex and she wanted him to know that.

Her slurps were longer and the head motions were going faster. Zakiya knew her head game drove Jarlath crazy and the sound of him being crazy over her drove her crazy so she sucked him like she only had one chance to do it.

Jarlath's phone lit up as it vibrated across the brown stand. "Hold baby, let me get this."

Ignoring his request, Zakiya kept sucking. She wanted to feel the numbness and she wasn't quite there yet.

Jarlath reached over to the stand to answer his phone. "Yo," Jarlath said, rubbing his free hand through Zakiya hair.

"Daddy, come and get me. They're going to let their big, big, dog bite me." Jarlath's heart felt as if it stopped, his eyes stared into the ceiling; his ears were ringing as if he had just heard a grenade go off.

"I got no time for bullshit. I want you and I want you bad. I'll call you back and tell you where you can meet me." The man on the phone hung up and Jarlath just laid there speechless as his dick softened and shrunk in Zakiya's mouth.

Curious, Zakiya looked up at Jarlath with her mouth ready to complain until she saw the expression on his face. "What's wrong baby? Who was that?" Zakiya asked, closing her robe and sitting up on the bed next to Jarlath while rubbing his chest. She looked him in the eyes and said,

"Baby, you are scaring me. Who was that, what's wrong?" Zakiya repeated.

Jarlath didn't want to scare her plus the last thing he needed on his mind at the time was a Zakiya crying asking him questions he didn't have the answer to. "Something came up, we can't go to Paris."

Zakiya poked her lips out like Naira. "Damn baby, it's always something. We will never get to spend time with each other if you don't learn how to say no to work." Zakiya got up walking towards the bathroom to wash her mouth with mouthwash.

"Put on your clothes, Zakiya, we got to go and now. I need to take you home; this can't wait."

Zakiya looked at Jarlath with a stressed face. "I tell you one thing if your ass don't change your ways, you are going to end up losing a good thing."

Zakiya's words were on repeat in Jarlath head. It was true he needed to change his ways, especially since he was now a family man but it wasn't that easy to do. He had to focus on the things he could do and that is make whoever responsible for the kidnapping of his angel pay.

Zakiya dressed quickly, she was ready to get home. Her plan was to ignore him for the rest of the week. She knew he hated her silence and she hated a man who didn't keep his word so that was going to make them even.

The ride home was a silent one. Jarlath's plan was to have his men check the house before they entered but as soon as the car stopped, Zakiya jumped out, slamming the door and racing inside. She opened the door and immediately she started shaking. The expression on her face said everything. No sounds exited her mouth. Zakiya's hands were in front her face like a clawed cat but she didn't touch her stiff mouth.

Jarlath came up behind Zakiya and wrapped his hands around her, holding on tight. He wasn't surprised to see Saran lying soaked in her own blood. "Baby go get in the car, go get in the car, Zakiya."

Zakiya stood still like a mannequin in a retail store, staring at Saran's shot body. The first word to come out of Zakiya mouth was, "WHY," she paused for ten seconds and asked the question again, WHY!"

"Come on Zakiya get in the car."

Zakiya shook Jarlath off, running upstairs to check to see if Naira's body was soaking in a puddle of blood upstairs, but she didn't find Naira nor did she see any blood. "Where is my baby, Jarlath? Where is my baby?" Zakiya screamed running back down the flared staircase. "Where is my baby?" she repeated, hitting him on the chest over and over again.

Zakiya wasn't getting any answer so she ran to Saran, kneeling down and dropping her tears on Saran's chest. "I'm so sorry, I'm so sorry, please forgive me friend."

"Yo, cover her body up," Jarlath said as he snatched Zakiya up in his arms and over his shoulders. She screamed out loudly, repeatedly, "I'm sorry friend,

I'm so sorry, Jarlath where is my baby, you better find my baby!" Jarlath ignored Zakiya and threw her in the SUV.